Dear Readers,

It's a fact: cowboy.

And, okay, I know I've got something of a reputation for writing romances featuring Navy SEALs, but truth be told, there's more than a little cowboy in every SEAL hero I've ever created. (After all, where do you think the phrase "cowboy up" comes from?)

But back in 1997, before Tom Paoletti and Stan Wolchonok, before Sam Starrett and Izzy Zanella, I wrote a book about a rancher named Cal Bartlett, who was a *real* cowboy.

There's something about a hardworking man who makes his living from the land, and Cal, the hero of *Forbidden*, does just that.

But Cal is not your everyday, average cowboy. His life was turned upside down when his parents died, leaving him responsible for his little brother, Liam. Throughout his life, Cal made countless sacrifices, working his tail off to give the kid an Ivy League education, putting his own hopes and dreams on the back burner. But, then, when Liam was coming into his own as a reporter, he was killed in war-torn San Salustiano.

Or so Cal was told.

Liam's former girlfriend, Kayla Grey, has never completely accepted Liam's death. And when she hears, from a San Salustiano refugee, a rumor about an Americano in a jungle prison...she travels from Boston to Montana to find the one person she knows will help her—Liam's big brother, Cal.

Sparks fly between the two before Kayla realizes that the tall cowboy with the ice-blue eyes is the man she's come to find.

True to form, Cal indeed cowboys up and goes to dangerous San Salustiano with Kayla, ready to kick down doors to find the truth—and maybe, hopefully, his little brother.

I'm delighted that Bantam has reissued Cal and Kayla's story—I hope you enjoy reading *Forbidden* as much as I enjoyed writing it!

Love,

Suzanne Brockmann

Suz Brockmann

Other Titles by Suzanne Brockmann

SUZANNE BROCKMANN

Forbidden

BANTAM BOOKS

FORBIDDEN
A Bantam Book

PUBLISHING HISTORY
Bantam Loveswept mass market edition published April 1997
Bantam mass market edition / October 2007

Published by
Bantam Dell
A Division of Random House, Inc.
New York, New York

This is a work of fiction. Names, characters, places, and incidents
either are the product of the author's imagination or are used
fictitiously. Any resemblance to actual persons, living or dead,
events, or locales is entirely coincidental.

ISBN 978-0-553-59092-0

Printed in the United States of America
Published simultaneously in Canada

www.bantamdell.com

OPM 10 9 8 7 6 5 4 3 2 1

For the Gaffney brothers,
Ed, Steve, and John

— 1 —

The storm came out of nowhere.

Or at least it seemed to. Mikayla Grey hadn't noticed the thunderously dark storm clouds as they filled the sky, but then, she had been preoccupied. By the time Kayla checked into the town's only guest house it was five o'clock and she was too tired to face the idea of driving out to the Bartlett ranch. She'd come out here instead, out into the wide open space of the countryside to get some fresh air, to take a walk on the rolling hills, and to gaze at the mountain range that loomed in the distance.

The truth was, Kayla was losing her momentum. She was starting to wonder exactly what on earth she was doing. She'd come all the way from Boston to Asylum, Montana, without even a phone call to announce her impending arrival, simply to talk to a man she'd never met before. And what she was going to tell him was going to sound crazy.

"Hi. I was a good friend of your brother Liam's. In fact, right before he died, he asked me to marry him. I know you probably don't understand why I didn't attend the memorial service you held for him two years ago, but you see, I couldn't admit that he was dead."

It had taken months—no, nearly an entire year—before Mikayla was able to acknowledge that Liam was not, indeed, ever coming back.

She had no idea of the reception Liam's older brother was going to give her. Liam had always spoken of the man ten years his senior with respect in his usually irreverent voice. Calvin Bartlett, Cal for short, was an odd mixture of father and brother to the younger man. Cal had raised Liam after their parents were killed in a car crash when Liam was five and Cal was fifteen. A grandfather had supposedly taken charge of the two boys, but according to Liam, the old man had been an invalid, barely able to care for himself, let alone a five-year-old.

Kayla looked up at the menacing clouds as the first fat drops of cold rain began to fall, blown sideways and upside down by great gusts of wind. Slowly at first, then faster and harder the rain fell, soaking her through her lightweight shirt and hiking shorts. Her shirt was a turtleneck, with a long row of tiny buttons down the front, but there were no sleeves, and the armholes were cut diagonally toward the neckline, exposing her shoulders. Shivering, Kayla picked up her pace, hurrying back the way she'd come, toward the town and the warmth of her room. But when she reached the crest of a hill, the driving rain obscured her vision, and she realized with a sinking heart that she no longer knew in which direction the town lay.

Her short blond hair was dripping into her eyes, and she pushed it out of her face as she turned in a slow circle. She'd climbed through the barbed-wire fencing that lined the road and had wandered away from town, assuming she'd simply be able to wander back.

She'd been wrong.

The wind blew harder, colder, and Kayla shivered again. At least it wasn't an electrical storm. At least there was no lightning.

Then a huge fork of lightning split the sky. Kayla dropped flat to the ground as the thunder roared around her.

She was in big, big trouble.

The phone rang.

Cal almost didn't hear it over the roar of the rain on the roof. And then when he did hear it, he wasn't so sure he wanted to answer it. These days the phone rang only when someone wanted something from him. And on a night like tonight, with the wind sending sheets of icy rain blowing slantwise across the hills, he'd just as soon not have anyone want anything from him.

But Thor lifted his head from between his front paws and gazed inquisitively at Cal with his brown, intelligent eyes. Aren't you going to answer the phone? the dog seemed to ask.

Cal picked it up. "Yeah."

"Good, you're there." It was Bob Monroe, the sheriff of Asylum.

"I am," Cal said. "Didn't you get that notice in your last phone bill, saying how it wasn't a good idea to make a phone call during an electrical storm?"

"Yeah, well, this is an emergency."

An emergency. Something told Cal he was about to get very, very wet. He was silent, waiting for Bob to go on.

"Tourist girl went out for a hike about an hour before the storm hit," Bob told him. "I just got a call from Ned over at the hotel, saying that she hasn't come back yet. She's out there somewhere, Cal, caught in the storm, probably lost."

"You want me to join one of the search parties," Cal said evenly. "All right. I'll be right—"

"No, no, son, I want you to *be* the search party," Bob interrupted. "You and that crazy dog of yours."

Cal didn't say a word. He just looked again out the window at the deluge and waited for the sheriff to explain.

"Lightning hit Matt Tucker's barn," Bob told him. "It was full of dry hay, and despite this rain, we've got damn near everyone in town working to keep the blaze from spreading to the house. I can't spare a single deputy, and Matt's neighbors aren't willing to leave him shorthanded either, not for some fool stranger who didn't have enough sense to stay indoors with a storm brewing." He paused. "That leaves you folks who live a bit outside of town, and unfortunately we've just had a report that the road washed out about a quarter mile past your place. You're it, Cal. You and Thor."

Cal glanced over at his dog. The animal's tail thumped and he seemed to smile. His ears were up, alert, as if he were listening to Bob's request for help.

"Anna Henrikson said she saw the girl out on one of your pastures," Bob continued. "We think she's probably still on your land."

"I got six hundred acres of land," Cal pointed out. He pulled the telephone's extension cord as far as it would go, taking it with him into the mud room. He pulled on his boots and shrugged into his long duster.

"I'm counting on you to find her," Bob said. "Weather report says this storm's gonna get worse before it gets better. We may even get an early snow. Dress warm and wear your hat, son."

"Right." Cal jammed his cowboy hat on his

head as he hung up the phone. He gave a whistle for Thor and stepped out the kitchen door and into the driving rain.

It had stopped thundering and lightning, but now there was ice mixed in with the rain. The wind howled and Kayla shivered uncontrollably. She was going to freeze to death. It was only September, technically still summer, yet she quite possibly was going to die of exposure.

But not if she could help it.

The side of the hill she was huddled against actually felt warm to the touch. Of course, anything would have felt warm to her—with her arms and legs bare and icy cold. But still, it gave her an idea.

She was carrying a pocketknife, and with freezing, fumbling fingers she pried the biggest blade open. She stabbed down at the sod, cutting the tough roots of the grass, exposing the dirt beneath.

The soil *was* warm. It had been sunny for most of the day. The sun had heated the earth, and it still retained that warmth.

Kayla dug. She used her knife, her hands, a rock she found. She tried to keep the sod intact, peeling it back from the dirt sort of like a blanket.

Exactly like a blanket.

The exertion should have been warming, but

the wind stole any heat from her body as it ripped past her.

The hole wasn't nearly big enough, but Kayla climbed into it anyway, curling into a ball. She refused to think about bugs and spiders and worms. She focused instead on the warmth of the soil as she covered herself with the sod and the dirt.

The possibility that she had just dug her own grave crossed her mind, but she pushed it away. Thinking that way wasn't going to get her any warmer. Thinking that way wasn't going to keep her alive.

Thor had found something.

Cal nudged his horse forward, peering through the curtain of rain that poured off the wide brim of his hat.

The dog barked again, dancing happily back and forth, leading Cal forward, unmindful of the tempest around them.

"What you got, boy?" Cal called, dismounting from his horse. He held tightly to the reins as he walked forward, well aware that his mount was skittish in this kind of weather. He couldn't blame the animal for wanting to make a beeline back to the warmth of the barn. Hell, *he* wanted to head straight to the barn himself.

Thor barked again, digging at the ground.

What the hell...?

A booted foot protruded from the earth. And a hand.

Sweet Jesus, they found the girl. She'd gone and dug herself under the sod!

Quickly, Cal hobbled his horse, then slid and skidded down the slick slope to where Thor was waiting.

He pushed back the grass and dirt, revealing drenched curls and a dirt-smeared face. She was shaking, shivering from the cold. Her eyes opened slowly, as if she were too cold to lift her lids.

She looked up at him. She had eyes the color of the hillside—green with flecks of gold and brown.

Cold. Her mouth formed the word, but she made no sound.

Thor was beside himself with happiness. "Good boy," Cal said to the dog as he pulled the girl up and out of the dirt. "Good dog."

Lord, underneath a layer of dirt, the girl was dressed in summer clothes—a light sleeveless top and a pair of ridiculously short shorts. He had to get her warm, but how? He was closer to town than he was to his ranch house. It was probably better to take her there anyway, in case she needed the doctor.

Cal drew her up into his arms. She was taller than he'd first thought from the way she'd been curled up under the sod. Her legs were impossibly long, her skin smooth and soft against his hands. When was the last time he'd touched a woman? Damned if he could remember. Not since the kid had died, and that had been two years ago this past summer.

Still holding the girl, Cal easily unhobbled his horse. Getting them both up and into the saddle was a different story. He had to sling her over his shoulder in a fireman's carry. Once on the horse, though, he positioned her in front of him, holding her close, wrapping his big duster around them both, ignoring the dirt that was smearing across his own clothes.

Cal dug his heels into his horse, heading at a gallop toward town.

It would take five minutes at the most. Five short minutes. But five minutes had never felt so blasted long. Cal tried his best to warm the girl. But he was starting to feel the chill of the rain and wind himself. He was trying not to think about how soft she felt against him, or the way she was burrowing her face into his chest, or the arm she'd weakly thrown around his neck, or those incredibly long, graceful legs.

Or the beautiful greenish-brown color of her eyes.

Cal reined in his horse at the southernmost gate of his ranch, unhooking it on horseback and pulling it shut after he and Thor went through. He took his horse more slowly on the paved road into town.

Cal could tell that Thor was mystified. He didn't know why his master was riding into town during a stormy evening. But he was a good-natured dog, and he trotted gamely alongside Cal's horse.

The rooming house was dark, but so was the rest of Main Street. The power had gone out. Still, Cal gave a shout for help as he slid down off his horse. He tossed the reins around a hitching bar and carried the girl up the wooden steps to the porch. The door was unlocked, so he pushed it open, bringing the girl inside. Thor followed, obediently curling up on the tile floor beside the door. Cal shut the door behind him with his foot.

"Ned!" he called. "Irma?"

There was no answer.

Dripping water and mud, he carried the girl down the hall to the kitchen. But the big room was empty, as was the dining room and the parlor.

"Is anyone here?"

There were no candles lit, even though Ned and Irma kept enough of them on hand. Power outages were frequent occurrences in Asylum, Montana. But the owners of the rooming house wouldn't have left candles burning if they weren't going to be around. And they weren't around.

There was no one here at all. They were all probably out at Tucker's, fighting the barn fire.

Cal picked up the telephone, but the line was dead.

It wasn't a big surprise. When the power went, the phone lines usually went too. So now what? He was still on his own. And he couldn't just leave the girl there. He had to figure out some way to get her warmed up.

A hot bath.

Ned's heating system ran on gas and solar power. He could run the girl a hot tub of water, warm her up that way.

Cal carried her up the stairs to the guest bedrooms. It didn't matter which one. He opened the first door he came to and brought the girl inside. He took her straight into the big bathroom and set her down on the floor. He peeled off his duster and wrapped it around her.

It was dark in there, but he got the water started running into the deep old-fashioned tub, sealing the drain with a stopper.

There was an array of candles on the wide counter that surrounded the sink. Cal found his matches and lit them all, and the room was filled with a golden glow. A thermostat on the wall controlled the little radiator that sat in the corner, and he turned the heat up as high as it would go, shutting the bathroom door to keep the warmth inside.

The girl was trying to untie her boot laces. She saw the tub, saw what he was intending to do, but her fingers weren't cooperating. Cal knelt down next to her.

"I'll get that," he said.

She nodded, pulling the duster more tightly around her.

Like a little kid, she'd double-knotted the laces of her boots. When Cal finally got them untied, he slipped them off her feet, pulling her socks off too.

Her feet and toes were so cold. He held them in his hands, trying to warm them. They weren't whitish-blue, thank God. She didn't look as if she were in any danger from frostbite.

As the water tumbled into the tub behind him, Cal glanced up at the girl. She was watching him.

"Thank you," she whispered,

"Let me help you into the water," he said.

She nodded again.

Cal helped her up, and she leaned heavily on him as, fully dressed, she stepped into the tub. He held on to her as she sank down into the warm water.

She leaned her head back against the rim of the tub and closed her eyes.

Now what? Cal didn't have a clue.

When the water in the tub rose dangerously high, he turned it off. The sudden silence was interrupted only by the sound of water that dripped from the faucet. Except it wasn't truly silent. He could hear the wind moaning outside the house. He could hear the splatter of icy rain as it blew against the windows. He could hear the girl's breathing—slow and steady—as she lay back in the tub.

He didn't want to leave her alone. It'd be a damn shame to save her from the storm only to have her drown in a bathtub. He gazed down at the girl, for the first time really allowing himself to take the time to look at her.

She wasn't as young as he'd thought. His first impression was that she was a college student, barely twenty years old. But he saw now that she was older. She was probably in her mid-twenties— but that was still young. Still a baby. He couldn't remember ever being that young.

Her hair was cut short—shorter even than his—up around her ears and in the back. The cut was boyish, but with her pretty, heart-shaped face, she looked nothing like a boy. Her neck was long and slender and incredibly feminine. Her hair was still wet, and it clung damp and dark like a cap against her head. It would be a lot lighter when it was dry. In fact, Cal would have bet all of next month's accounts receivable that this girl was a blonde.

She *was* very pretty, with fine, delicate features—wide cheekbones, small nose, slightly pointed chin. She looked fragile lying there with her eyes closed, long lashes dark against her pale cheeks.

In general, Cal didn't like blondes. And he didn't go for fragile-looking girls. He liked women he could hold on to. Substantial women, not delicate flowers.

No, this girl was definitely not his type.

So why was he standing there, staring at her, imagining how beautiful she must look with her eyes open and a smile on her face?

Cal pulled his eyes away from her, and came face-to-face with his own reflection in the mirror over the sink. Damn, he was a mess. His clothes were covered with mud, and his shirt was soaked. His dark hair was dented from his hat, and the shadows and flickering candlelight made his lean face look harsh and stern. His eyes appeared pale and colorless, as if the blue had faded away. Maybe it had. God knows, he couldn't remember the last time he'd smiled.

He rearranged his face, pushing his mouth up into a grin. It felt odd, as if his muscles were rusty, and it looked even odder. It made him smile ruefully, with a slight twisting of his lips. That was a little better, but not much.

He wasn't a bad-looking guy. At six feet six, with a hardworking rancher's well-muscled, lean body, he cut an imposing figure. And he may not have had a pretty face, not the way Liam had anyway, but his dark hair, faintly Native American features, and blue gray eyes made for a striking combination. Or so he'd been told.

So why was it that he'd spent most of his thirty-seven years alone?

That was a damn good question.

Cal washed up in the sink, pulling the tails of his soaked and muddied shirt from his pants. He took the shirt off and wrapped a towel around his shoulders. His pants were just as wet, but they would have to wait. Wrapping the towel more securely around him, he quietly went out of the bathroom and started a fire in the attached bedroom's big fireplace. It didn't take long before flames were snapping and crackling in the hearth. Then he went back into the bathroom to check on the girl. She hadn't moved.

Cal sat down on the closed seat of the commode to wait for her to open her eyes.

— 2 —

Kayla was finally starting to feel warm. She heard the sound of water being let out of the tub and felt warmer water being run in. She opened her eyes and saw the cowboy dip his fingers in the water pouring out of the faucet, testing its temperature. He'd taken off his shirt, and his smooth skin gleamed golden tan in the light from the candles. His muscles moved under his skin as he reached forward to turn off the flow, and he straightened back up, wiping his wet fingers on a crisp white towel.

He was a giant. Dear God, he had to be well over six feet. He seemed to fill the tiny bathroom, making Kayla feel positively petite. And at her own five feet eleven, it wasn't often she felt that way.

That was when he noticed that her eyes were open. Their gazes met and he froze.

The cowboy's eyes were the lightest shade of

blue-gray Kayla had ever seen. Or maybe they just seemed that way in contrast to his tanned face and the jet-black hair that tumbled over his forehead.

His face was rugged, his features angular—craggy and weather-beaten. He had wide, exotic cheekbones, lean cheeks, and a big, slightly hooked nose. His eyebrows were thick and dark, and his eyes could be described only as flinty.

Kayla's gaze dropped lower, to the well-defined muscles of his shoulders and chest. His body looked hard. He looked as if it would hurt to bump into him.

But Kayla knew he'd carried her back here, back to the guest house. Much of what she remembered was foggy, but she *did* remember that his arms had been gentle.

As the rain pounded against the roof, she also remembered a wet nose, a furry face, and inquisitive, friendly brown eyes.

"Is your dog inside?" she asked. Her voice sounded raspy and hoarse.

"Thor?" The cowboy nodded. "He's waiting down by the door. He was even muddier than you were. And he knows it too. He won't dare come upstairs."

His deep voice was pure Montana—soft and rich with a slow western drawl.

"I got you pretty dirty too," Kayla said. His jeans were soaked and streaked with mud.

"Nothing a load of laundry and a shower won't cure."

It was more than the color of his eyes that was odd, Kayla thought as she gazed up at him. It was his lack of expression that was so strange. There was a matter-of-fact detachment in his eyes, as if he kept himself carefully distanced from any and everything.

He seemed particularly distanced from the fact that he was standing in the bathroom, half dressed, while she was in the tub. Of course, she still had her clothes on. But that didn't make it any less weird. It was oddly, quietly intimate with the candlelight and the wind howling outside. But he seemed not to notice.

"What were you doing anyway, wandering around out there?" he asked.

"That's exactly what I was doing," she replied. "Wandering. I wanted some fresh air."

He almost smiled. "Guess you got some."

Kayla did smile at that. "I got way more than I bargained for."

Cal gazed down at her, held in place by her smile. It was wide and uninhibited, and it lit up her entire face, making her eyes crinkle at the edges. Something moved deep within him, something that hadn't stirred in a long, long time.

"I'm not from around here." The girl smiled

again. "But you probably already guessed that, right?"

Cal nodded.

"It's still summer back east, where I'm from," she said.

"It's still summer here too."

"You could've fooled me. You and Thor saved me from a cold, miserable night. I owe you both a steak dinner."

"Next time, pay attention to the weather before you go out," Cal told her. He turned away slightly, afraid she might think he was staring at her. Which he had been. Damn, she was pretty.

"There's not going to be a next time," she said melodramatically. "From now on I'm sticking to my car."

"You'll miss a lot that way." He glanced back at her.

"Yeah, like freezing to death." She tipped her head back under the water and rinsed the silt from her hair. "Or trying to impersonate a prairie dog."

"That was real smart to do that—to dig into the ground." Cal watched her sit back up and sweep the water from her hair. He knew he was staring again, but he couldn't help it. "It probably kept your body temperature from dropping too low."

"I remembered that pioneers used to make houses out of sod," the girl told him. "There was no other shelter out there...." She shrugged and smiled again. "I'm serious about that steak dinner. I'd like to pay you back—you've gone to a lot of trouble for me."

Her smile was like sunshine. And when Cal opened has mouth to tell her there was no need to repay him for anything, he found himself saying something entirely different.

"All right."

"Tomorrow night?" she asked, gazing up at him with those green eyes. "Say...about seven o'clock?"

Cal nodded. "Yeah."

Sweet Lord, he had a dinner date for tomorrow night. And he was actually looking forward to it. At least, he thought that was what this odd feeling in his gut was. It had been so long since he'd felt anything at all....

Kayla pulled her gaze away from the cowboy's. He was going to have dinner with her tomorrow night. It meant nothing, she tried to tell herself. It wasn't really a date. It was a thank-you in the form of a meal. The fact that something subtle had changed in his eyes wasn't anything to worry about. She glanced up at him again, and sure enough, the heat in his eyes was still there, making her feel for the briefest of moments as if *she* were the promised meal.

But he quickly looked away, as if he were too well mannered to let her see his attraction to her.

And when he looked back again, his eyes were once more expressionless. His feelings were still there though—he was simply hiding them.

Their attraction was a mutual thing, Kayla realized. Maybe it was his western accent, reminding her of Liam. Except Liam's accent had been faint, barely there, worn down by his years in Boston, by his desire to fit in with the fast-paced city's way of life. This cowboy's accent, though, was thick and rich and resonant, surrounding her like the warm wool of a hand-knit sweater.

Physically, the cowboy was nothing like Liam. Liam had been barely taller than she was. He had been slender and blond and quick to smile. His eyes had been blue too, but they were the color of the summer sky, not icicle blue like the cowboy's.

It was natural that Kayla should feel some sort of fondness for this man, she tried to reassure herself. After all, he'd rescued her from the storm. He'd heroically carried her here. He'd stayed with her, cared for her. And it certainly didn't hurt that his sternly handsome face and his well-proportioned physique made him look like the poster model for the untamed West.

Kayla glanced down at her hands. Her fingers were raw from the digging she'd done, and starting to sting. "I'm turning into a prune," she told the cowboy. "I've got to get out of the tub."

He moved closer as she stood, ready to catch her if she slipped.

His presence was oddly reassuring. It was odd because, with her track record, living in the city the way she did, and working full-time for the Boston Women's Crisis Center, Kayla couldn't remember the last time she'd felt anything but uneasy from the attention of a strange man. Or even a familiar man. And this cowboy was no lightweight. With his height and build, he didn't have to say please and thank you to get what he wanted. Still, Kayla felt no threat from him.

She wobbled slightly, and he gently took hold of her arm.

"Let me give you a hand," he said. His voice sounded tighter, choked, and as Kayla glanced at him, following his gaze, she instantly knew why.

Her wet clothes clung to her intimately. The normally thick white cotton of her shirt was made almost transparent from its wetness. And with the cutaway shoulders of this shirt, she wasn't wearing a bra. She might as well have been standing in front of him barebreasted.

The cowboy was trying his best not to stare. He looked away, down at the floor, but not before Kayla saw a flare of heat in his ice-blue eyes.

Still, he was almost as embarrassed as she was. He took a big towel from the rack on the wall and wrapped it quickly around Kayla's shoulders.

"Better get out of those wet things," he said gruffly. He motioned to the door with his head. "I'll be in the other room if you need me."

Cal gently closed the bathroom door behind him, letting out a long-held breath.

Damn.

Damn.

The powers that be surely had some reason for putting Cal in a situation like that, but he sure as hell hadn't figured that reason out yet. He knew nothing about this girl. For all he knew, she was married. The only things he knew about her for sure were that she was a fighter, that she had the prettiest smile he'd ever seen, and that she had a body to die for. Hell, he didn't even know her name.

He crossed to the fire, crouched on the rug in front of it, and threw another log on the flames.

The bathroom door opened with a creak, and Cal looked up to see the girl peeking out.

"I'm sorry," she said, a tinge of embarrassment on her cheeks. "I know this is awkward, but . . . I need your help with these buttons on my shirt. . . ." Cal stood as she crossed toward him, toward the light of the fire. She held out her hands in explanation. "My fingers are still kind of numb."

She'd also torn up her hands digging that hole he'd found her in. The tips of her fingers looked raw and scraped and very painful.

She shivered, and Cal drew her closer to the fire. There were about two dozen tiny buttons starting at the high neck of the shirt that still clung revealingly to her body. Cal tried to pay attention only to those little buttons as he began unfastening them. He tried not to think about the fact that her breasts were mere millimeters from his fingers.

"I'm sorry," the girl whispered again. Her face was close to his own, and he glanced into her eyes. "I really couldn't get these buttons. I don't want you to think that this is some kind of come-on or something, because it's not."

"Yeah, I know," he said, his voice nothing but a whisper too.

Each button he unfastened revealed a little more of her soft, pale skin. The firelight flickered, creating a romantic glow. It was the perfect ambiance for undressing a lover. But this girl wasn't his lover.

At least not yet.

But maybe after dinner tomorrow night . . .

Kayla closed her eyes, feeling the cowboy's work-roughened fingers unbutton her shirt. His knuckles brushed against her and he murmured an apology.

Desire was a funny thing. It had been *years* since she'd as much as glanced twice at a good-looking man. Yet here she was, alone in a firelit room with some cowboy, and her body was giving her signals she hadn't felt in ages.

If she swayed toward him, if their lips met, Kayla knew he would kiss her. And that kiss would lead to other kisses, and more...The attraction that sparked between them would follow through to its natural course.

And no one would ever have to know—no one but Kayla and this cowboy.

Whose name she didn't even know. Dear God, she was actually considering having a one-night stand with Asylum, Montana's, version of Wyatt Earp.

No. She wasn't truly considering it. She knew exactly what would happen if she so much as tried. He would kiss her, and she would kiss him. It would feel nice—more than nice—and she'd think that maybe this time was going to be different. And then it would happen. The fear would slam down around her and she would push him away.

"Do you..." The cowboy cleared his throat. "Do you want me to get the...this other button too?"

Kayla opened her eyes. He was talking about the button at the waist of her shorts. "Do you mind?"

He smiled then, a fierce, hot smile that actually warmed his eyes and took a solid five years off his

stern face. "Lady, there's some things I mind doing, but undressing a woman is not one of 'em."

He unfastened the button, his knuckles warm
against her chilled belly. His eyes were still
amused as he glanced at her again. "Shoot, I'm going to get *years* of fantasies out of this one."

Kayla had to smile. "You mean, like, 'Dear
Penthouse: You won't believe what I found under
the sod out in the back forty..'"

The cowboy actually laughed aloud. "Something like that." His dark good looks were accentu-
ated when he smiled, but when he laughed, he was
totally off the scale. "I don't suppose you need any
additional help...?"

Wordlessly, Kayla shook her head.

"What room are you really in?" he asked.

"I think it's number three."

"I'll go get your suitcase—you *do* have something warm you can put on, don't you?"

Kayla nodded.

"Good." He started toward the door to the hallway. "In the meantime, get out of those wet things,
wrap yourself in a blanket, and huddle close to
the fire."

But the sight of thick, damp snow swirling
around outside the window caught Kayla's full attention. "My God!"

The cowboy turned back, ready to come to her
rescue again if need be. "You all right?"

"It's snowing," Kayla said inanely. She turned to stare at the cowboy. It was September 18, and it was *snowing*.

"First snowfall of the year," he told her. "From the looks of it, we'll get a dusting—no more 'n six inches."

"Six inches." Six inches of snow was going to fall tonight. That wasn't a dusting. That was a major snowfall. At least it was where she came from. "If you hadn't found me, I would've been buried under six inches of snow?"

"Probably."

"I would've died," Kayla said, the realization hitting her hard in the stomach. "I would've been frozen to death."

He nodded. "Wearing what you're wearing—yeah."

"You saved my life tonight."

The cowboy thought about it for a half a second. "Yes, ma'am," he said. Turning, he left the room.

When Cal carried the suitcase back into the room, the girl had wrapped herself in one of the blankets from the bed and was lying on the rug in front of the fire. Her eyes were closed, and Cal moved quickly toward her, setting her case down on the floor and kneeling next to her.

He touched the side of her face and her eyes opened.

"You okay?"

"Just resting." She smiled wanly. "I feel a little bit like I've been hit by a truck, but I'm okay."

Cal nodded. She was okay. When he came in and saw her lying there...His heart was pounding. But, damn! Four hours ago he didn't even know that his heart was in any kind of working order.

The girl struggled to sit up, and the blanket slipped off one smooth, pale shoulder before she gathered it more tightly around her.

As they sat on the floor in front of the fire, Cal fought the urge to touch her face again. Her skin had felt so smooth, so soft beneath his fingers. He could reach out, touch her cheek, cup her chin, pull her mouth up toward his and...

"I'm feeling a little off balance," she admitted, staring into the fire. "When I was out there and the wind started blowing, and it was raining and cold...I was afraid I might be killed, but I didn't really, *honestly* believe it could happen. I mean, to think that I could go out for a walk and end up dead..."

She turned and gazed unsmilingly at him, her eyes wide. Her curls had dried, and she *was* a blonde. Her hair gleamed golden in the firelight.

She was right. She could very well have died. If

the sheriff hadn't called, if Cal hadn't gone out into the storm, if he hadn't searched the eastern pasture, if Thor hadn't had such a good nose... She would have died, and he would have helped bring her body back into town, marveling at the foolishness of her lightweight summer clothes, unaware that she had a smile that could have warmed even his glacial heart.

He simply would never have known.

"Would you mind very much," she asked almost inaudibly, "putting your arms around me?"

Cal shook his head. "No, ma'am." He shifted closer, drawing her into his arms, feeling a rush of emotion, of relief, of thankfulness. She *hadn't* died. Whoever she was, wherever she'd come from, he'd found her and now she was warm and safe and alive. And in his arms.

He had to close his eyes for a moment, nearly overcome by the sensation of her soft body, by the sweet scent of her hair. She leaned her head against his shoulder, gazing into the fire.

Cal's heart was beating so loudly, he was convinced she'd be able to hear it. "I don't suppose *this* is a come-on," he said huskily, half teasing, half hopeful.

He felt more than heard her laugh. "Not a chance," she said. "I just needed a hug."

He'd needed a hug too, Cal realized. He'd needed something like this for the past two years.

Longer. He'd needed a hug since he'd been pulled out of class at age fifteen and told by his school principal that his father and stepmother had been killed in a car accident on Route 16.

"You could've ridden right past me," the girl said. Her voice sounded sleepy.

It took Cal a moment to figure out that she was still talking about the way he had found her out in the field.

"I might've." Cal leaned his cheek gently against the top of her head. He might have, but he hadn't. "But Thor wouldn't have missed you."

"Thor," she said. "As in the god of thunder?"

"Thor as in Henry David Thoreau. You know, the American philosopher?"

She lifted her head and looked up at him. "You're kidding."

"No, ma'am."

They were nose to nose, or—more important— mouth to mouth. Her lips were only a whisper away from his, and he lowered his head, covering her mouth with his before he allowed himself time to think.

She tasted so sweet, and her lips were so soft. She made a soft mewing sound in her throat, a sound of surprise—and of pleasure. She hesitated for a second, and he would have pulled away, but then she opened her mouth to him, looping her arms up and around his neck. He deepened the kiss instantly, sweeping his tongue into her mouth, and she responded, welcoming him.

Cal was delirious with pleasure and dizzy with need, and he forced himself to pull back, to take his time, for fear of overwhelming her. He kissed her again and again, long, slow, deep, lazy kisses that drove him half mad with desire. He ran his fingers down the slender length of one of her arms, and she shivered, but this time it was not from the cold. He pushed the blanket down, away from her, and the firelight gleamed and flickered across her bare skin. As he kissed her again, he touched her—her neck, her shoulders, her back, all the way down to the soft, smooth curve of her waist. Her skin was like silk beneath his fingers, so warm and soft and smooth.

He felt so incredibly alive.

He filled his hand with the firm weight of her breast, running his thumb across her taut nipple, across the place where he would have damn near sold his soul to touch with his mouth, his lips, his tongue.

He lifted his head to do just that, but she pulled back, away from him, gathering the blanket back around her.

She was breathing as raggedly as he was.

Her eyes were wide and her mouth looked swollen from his kisses, from the burn of his stubble. He hadn't shaved before leaving the house this evening. He hadn't known . . .

There was shock in her eyes. And embarrassment. And even a little bit of fear. And Cal knew that he'd pushed too hard, gone too far. She wasn't going to have sex with him. Not tonight. But oddly enough, that didn't matter. It didn't matter half as much as getting her to smile at him again.

"That *was* a come-on, in case you were wondering," he told her.

He'd wanted to make her smile, and she did. It was low wattage, but better than nothing. "I figured as much." She looked away from him, down at the floor, into the fire, still clutching the blanket tightly around her. "We don't even know each other. And I'm . . ."

Kayla glanced back at the cowboy, still sitting next to her on the rug in front of the fire. He was watching her intently, firelight playing across his chiseled features, glimmering over his powerful-looking chest and washboard stomach, gleaming in his shining black hair, reflecting in his pale blue eyes.

Another man wouldn't have let her push him away. Another man would've been on top of her, pressing his advantage, not taking no for an answer. Another man would've taken the entire situation for an invitation. Another man wouldn't have such a fascinating mix of apology and desire lighting his eyes, mirrored in his face, and in the careful way he used his body language to offer her both respect and a willingness to wait for her signal to continue.

What would he think if she told him the truth—that she'd been with a man who hadn't taken no for an answer?

"I'm not interested in casual sex," she said instead. "I mean, really, you don't even know my name."

"We could change *that* real fast." The passion in his eyes was nearly overwhelming. How could she have thought his eyes were icy or expressionless? The burning heat she could see there now was the furthest thing from cold she'd ever seen.

What had she been thinking, kissing this stranger that way? My God, she'd kissed him with such abandon, such hunger, she'd absolutely shocked herself. She'd never kissed anyone like that before.

Maybe it was knowing that she could have died. Maybe it was gratitude—after all, he'd saved her life.

She gazed into the cowboy's eyes, trying to see what it was about him that made her drop all her defenses so utterly. What she saw there only confused her more. He was a stranger, she knew that, but there was something in his eyes that seemed so familiar, as if she'd somehow known him all her life.

"Are you going to tell me your name?" he asked, a small smile playing about the corners of his elegantly shaped lips. "Or do you want me to go first and tell you mine?"

"Kayla," she said breathlessly. "My name's Kayla."

"Kayla," he repeated. "That's pretty. Pleased to meet you, Kayla."

Their gazes met and held, and held and held. He slowly leaned forward to kiss her again, giving her plenty of time to back away. But, hypnotized, Kayla couldn't move. Maybe this time would be different. Maybe this time she wouldn't feel smothered by the fear. Maybe...

Downstairs, the front door banged open, and the cowboy lifted his head sharply.

A voice carried up the stairs. "Bart, that your horse outside? Oh, hey, Thor. Hey, buddy. Where's your boss, huh, boy? Is he upstairs?"

In one swift, catlike movement, the cowboy was up on his feet and moving quickly into the bathroom. Bart. His name was Bart.

He came out of the bathroom a moment later, swiftly buttoning up his wet and muddy shirt, tucking the tails into his pants. He didn't want her found in a compromising position, Kayla realized. He didn't want anyone to find him there, with her, in front of the fire, without his shirt on. It was incredibly sweet.

Unless, of course, he was married and it was *himself* he didn't want found in a compromising position...

Ned, the owner of the guest house, appeared in the door, glancing from Kayla to the cowboy. Bart.

"You found her," he said with relief in his voice. "Thank goodness." He looked at Kayla. "You hurt, miss? You need a visit from Doc Samuelson?"

Kayla shook her head. "No, I'm all right. I'm just going to go to bed." Alone. She glanced at the cowboy. He was still watching her, and although his expression didn't change, she knew he could easily read her mind.

"Just holler if you need anything," Ned said, turning away.

"Sorry about getting your floors all dirty," the cowboy called after him.

"I'll take dirty floors over a dead guest any day," Ned called back cheerfully.

The cowboy hadn't moved from his position in the center of the room. He stood there, gazing at her, hunger still gleaming in his eyes. Kayla pulled herself to her feet, wobbling slightly, and he was beside her in a flash.

"Need help getting into bed?" he asked.

Kayla had to smile. "Somehow, I mistrust your motivation," she said. "I get the feeling that you're no longer solely trying for your Helping Hand cub scout merit badge."

He smiled as he pulled back the sheets and covers. "No, Kayla," he said, her name like music with his warm western drawl, "you're right. I've definitely got an ulterior motive here. But right now I promise I won't do anything more than tuck you in, kiss you good night, and close the door tightly behind me when I leave. It's tomorrow night you're going to have to worry about."

Still wrapped tightly in the blanket, Kayla climbed into the bed. Tomorrow night. As he drew the other bed coverings up to her chin, she closed her eyes, physically and emotionally exhausted. Tomorrow night was a million years away. And right now all she wanted to do was sleep.

She felt his lips brush hers in the gentlest of good-night kisses. She felt him move back, away from the bed, and heard him go into the bathroom—probably to get his long, dirty duster from where she'd left it on the tile floor.

He paused before he went out the door. "I never told you *my* name," he said quietly.

"Ned called you Bart," Kayla murmured, not even opening her eyes. "Good night, Bart." She'd deal with this cowboy tomorrow. She'd tell him the truth. She had every right to be gunshy, so to speak. She'd make him understand that she wasn't ready for the kind of casual relationship he so clearly wanted. She would probably never be. She'd tell him about Liam too, explain why she would be leaving town almost right away. He probably knew Liam. In a town this size, everyone must've known Liam. . . .

"Bart's just a nickname," the cowboy said. "It's short for Bartlett. Cal Bartlett."

He closed the door behind him with a quiet click as Kayla's eyes opened.

She sat up in the bed, suddenly wide awake.

Cal Bartlett. Cal *Bartlett* . . . ?

Dear God, the cowboy was Liam's older brother.

—3—

"Cal Bartlett! This is a surprise. What brings you into the store this morning?"

Cal gazed across the racks of clothing at Marge Driscoll's smiling face. He was ready for her question. He'd come prepared. He knew it was impossible to go into Driscoll's without getting the third degree.

"New pair of jeans," he told her. "Tore the knees out of a pair last week. Need some socks too. Half a dozen pairs or so. Wool. For winter."

"I thought you were joining your ranch hands up at the north pasture," Marge said, taking several packs of her warmest, largest socks from the drawers behind the counter. "Andy told me you were going to take that fancy little airplane of yours up to meet them today."

"Change of plans," Cal said evenly. He'd called Earl Wayne, his foreman, first thing that morning to let him know he wouldn't be arriving for another day or two. Earl had assured Cal he had the herd well under control He'd even urged his boss to take advantage of the situation and take a well-earned trip someplace warm and exotic. Mexico. The Caribbean. Hawaii. Spend a small portion of that money Cal worked such long, hard hours to bring in.

Cal knew exactly where he wanted to go, and it wasn't but a few hundred yards from where he was standing. In fact, if he turned his head, he'd be able to see down the road clear to the sign for Ned's Guest House and Restaurant. Where Kayla was staying.

He pulled a pair of jeans in his size down from the shelf. He'd been buying this size and length in this brand for so long, he didn't need to think about trying them on. They fit. He knew they fit.

As he carried the jeans across the store toward the cash register, he stopped at a rack of shirts. They were long-sleeved with buttons down the front, in an amazing array of both bright and muted colors. They were cotton—stone-washed, the tag said. As he touched them, he was surprised by their softness. They felt like butter beneath his fingers.

This was really why he'd gone into Driscoll's that morning. He wanted a new shirt to wear out to dinner with Kayla that night. Everything in his closet was either badly worn out or much too formal.

"That blue will look really good on you," Marge called across the room. "I think I saw at least one in your size too."

Cal had been looking at a shirt that was light brown, but now he pulled out the blue. It was neither navy nor pale, but rather a deep, rich shade of royal blue. It looked like the color of the sky directly overhead on a perfect, cloudless autumn day. He'd never owned an article of clothing that was so colorful in his entire life.

He carried it over to the counter with the jeans. His entire life was due for a change.

Cal had woken up that morning with only one thing on his mind: Kayla. He was going to see her again that night. He was going to have dinner with her, gaze into her exquisitely shaped green eyes, and do his damnedest to wind up back in her room at the guest house after dinner was over. Or he could bring her back to the ranch. There was no one else around—all his hired hands were driving his herd up north. He had the whole place to himself. Kayla could stay with him as long as she liked.

Cal could feel anticipation coursing through his veins. It was an odd sensation—and one he certainly hadn't felt in a long time. Certainly not since that awful day he'd received the news that Liam had died.

Two years. For two years he'd pulled himself out of bed with no sense of wonder as to what the day would bring. He'd gone through the motions, gotten the job done. He'd wake up from the night-time confusion that sleep and dreams brought, and the reality that his kid brother was dead and buried would come crashing down on him, numbing him.

That morning the same truth awaited him. Liam was still dead. He was still never coming back. But somehow it was the tiniest bit easier to bear.

The kid had died doing something he believed in. He'd died trying to make a difference in people's lives. He'd lived hard and fast and exuberantly. Cal could respect that. For the first time, he could begin to imagine being at peace with that.

He still missed Liam. He always would. He'd carry his regrets for his brother's young life cut short to his own grave.

Liam's life was over, but Cal's wasn't. For two years Cal had wished he'd been the one who'd died. But that morning Cal had woken up and realized that he was glad—*damn* glad—to be alive.

Last night he'd pulled a girl out from under the sod of a hillside. Last night she'd gazed up into his eyes, and with a smile like a new morning's sunshine, she'd somehow, miraculously, jump-started his heart.

He didn't even know this girl, he tried to tell himself. Hell, he didn't even know her last name. She was too young, too pretty, too good to be true.

But there he was, buying himself a new bright-blue shirt to wear the next time he saw her. It seemed ludicrous and foolish, and he almost put the shirt back on the rack. But Marge took it out of his hands and rung it up on her ancient cash register.

"I heard you were busy last night," she said, glancing slyly up at him, "rescuing our sweet young visitor from some northeastern city?"

"Yep." Cal said nothing more, steadily meeting Marge's eyes. He handed her a hundred-dollar bill.

She knew him well enough not to push. Instead of commenting further, she gave him his change and his purchases, neatly packed in a paper bag. "Have a good one," she said with a smile.

Cal nodded his farewell and jammed his hat back onto his head as he stepped out of the store and onto the sidewalk. Most of the previous night's snow had already melted, particularly in town. He tossed the bag into the front seat of his truck, then crossed around to the driver's side.

"Ho there, Calvin. What you doing in town in the middle of a workday, son? Buying some new duds from Driscoll's, huh? Now, let me guess . . . Could that possibly be because of a woman?"

Cal turned to see old Doc Samuelson grinning at him from the sidewalk. "Just running some errands," Cal said calmly, fighting the urge to scowl. He knew how interested the good folk of Asylum were in *any* tidbit of gossip. He could just imagine the speculation that had gone on concerning himself and the city girl. Clearly the story of his rescue of the girl had already spread like wildfire. The local romantics—of which there were quite a few, the elderly doctor included—probably had the two of them paired off and ready to march down the aisle.

"Herd's up at winter pasture," Cal continued. "I'll be joining them after the weekend."

"You're taking a few days off, are you?" Doc smiled. "Good, good. It's about time you had a break. Where you heading now? Home, I hope. And step on it, son."

Cal lifted an eyebrow, but he didn't have to ask why.

Doc Samuelson explained. "I just gave directions out to your ranch to the prettiest girl to hit town since Mrs. S. arrived in the back of her daddy's truck fifty years ago. She seemed real anxious to talk to you."

Kayla. Doc had to be talking about Kayla. Cal turned to open the door of his truck, suddenly eager to get home. Kayla—waiting for him out at the ranch. And this time he'd shaved. . . .

"I asked her why the rush, and she said something about Liam," Doc continued. "Maybe I've got this wrong, but I think this pretty girl was a friend of your brother's."

Cal froze. He felt himself go entirely still. His heart was still beating, but other than that he didn't move, didn't breathe, didn't even think. Somehow he managed to speak. "Come again?"

"From what she told me," Doc repeated cheerfully, "it sounds as if she knew Liam real well. She seems like a real nice girl—figures Liam would've gotten himself hooked up to a girl who had more than just a pretty face and generous curves."

Kayla—Liam's fiancée? No, not fiancée. Liam had asked a girl to marry him—he'd told Cal about it right before he'd left on his last trip—but she'd never agreed, never said yes. Apparently she hadn't cared enough even to show up for the kid's memorial service. Why the hell would she show up now?

"You're sure she mentioned Liam?" Cal asked. Maybe the town doctor misheard. The girl his little brother had fallen for was named Michelle or something like that. Not Kayla.

"Absolutely. She was wearing his rodeo ring on a chain around her neck," Doc said. He chuckled. "Remember that big old thing with the inset garnet the size of Butte? Remember when he won that—damn near scared you to death. He was only sixteen at the time."

Cal nodded. He remembered. He'd searched for the ring among Liam's things that had been shipped back from Boston. He'd never found it.

"I better get home." He climbed into the truck, praying that Doc was wrong, praying that it wouldn't be Kayla waiting there for him.

Doc waved, and Cal started the engine with a roar. As he drove the bumpy road back to his ranch, he couldn't shake the feeling that he knew exactly what he was going to find when he got home. He was going to find Kayla's car parked alongside his house, with Kayla sitting in the sun, on the hood.

He pulled into his dirt driveway, his tires scrambling for traction in the mud.

Please, God, let me be wrong.

Kayla.

The sun gleamed off her golden hair as she sat on the steps leading up to his porch, Thor's head on her lap. Thor scrambled to his feet as the truck approached, and Kayla straightened up too, encircling her knees with her arms.

The very last of the promise and anticipation Cal had been feeling earlier that morning vanished in a wave of disappointment and anger. He braked to a stop in front of the house, and the bag that held his new shirt skidded off the seat and onto the floor. Cal didn't bother to pick it up.

Kayla didn't say a word. She just watched him as he climbed out of the truck, as he crossed around to stand in front of her.

"Your name isn't really Kayla," he said. His voice didn't come out as even and calm as he might have wished. His throat was raspy and he sounded a touch hoarse. He crossed his arms and cleared his throat.

"It's a nickname," she admitted. "Short for Mikayla."

Mikayla. That was it. Mikayla Grey. Cal remembered now. "You . . . knew my brother."

Kayla nodded. "Yeah, I did."

She was wearing Liam's old rodeo ring around her neck on a thick gold chain, just as Doc described. She hadn't been wearing it the night before. Cal wouldn't have missed it. He *couldn't* have.

Cal climbed the steps to the porch. "You were his girlfriend. He wanted to marry you. And you didn't even bother to see him buried."

He knew she could clearly read the anger in his eyes. Her face looked pale, her own eyes wide, her lips set. Still, she managed to look impossibly pretty.

"You didn't see him buried either," she countered, her chin held high. "There was nothing left to bury."

"It was a ceremony," Cal retorted. "A ritual designed for the survivors to pay *respect* to the dead."

"I couldn't do it," Kayla said. Her green eyes were swimming in tears. Cal had to turn away. "It was too soon." There was a catch in her voice, and Cal knew that her tears had slipped down her face. "I couldn't believe that he was really gone. I felt if I'd come out here, to his memorial service, I would somehow be betraying him. And that would have been the ultimate *disrespect*."

Cal sat down heavily on the steps, pushing back his hat and rubbing his forehead with one hand. That was some eloquent excuse. Betrayal. Disrespect. The real truth was that she hadn't had the time or inclination to travel halfway across the country to say good-bye to a man who had loved her enough to want to marry her.

Whimpering softly, Thor pushed his head up and into Cal's other hand. Tiredly rubbing the dog's ears, Cal glanced at Kayla. She was wiping her face with the heels of her hands, as if she didn't want him to see her tears. His heart clenched as he gazed at her, and he honestly had to ask himself whether his anger truly was derived from his displeasure that Kayla—Mikayla Grey—hadn't attended Liam's funeral, or because this girl that he wanted so very badly had once belonged, heart, body, and soul, to Liam.

Whether she deserved it or not, she'd been his brother's beloved.

Somehow that knowledge made Cal's own desire and his intense physical attraction to her seem lewd and much less than pristine.

Liam was dead, and Cal had spent much of the night before and all of that day dreaming up ways to get his brother's lover into his own bed. Damn, but that made him mad. Mad at himself—mad at her, too, for making him want her. And mad at the kid for going and dying in the first place.

Cal took out his checkbook. "How much do you want?" he asked flatly.

"Excuse me?" She stared at him—as if she didn't know damn well what he was talking about.

"Money," he said. "You're here for money, right? How much do you need?"

Her gaze narrowed. "God, you're a bastard."

"Round it up to the nearest thousand," Cal told her bluntly. "Then take the damn check and get the hell off my land."

Kayla stood up. "I'm not here for your lousy money!"

"Then why the hell *are* you here?!"

"Because I need your help," she spat back at him. "Because I think that Liam might still be alive."

—4—

Kayla saw pure, molten rage in Cal Bartlett's pale gray eyes, and for one terrifying second she thought the man was going to raise his hand and strike her. But then the light in his eyes flickered and went out, taking with it all the emotion on his face.

When he spoke, he matter-of-factly uttered a crude, anatomically impossible phrase that told her with absolutely no doubt exactly what she should do. "Get off my ranch," he added with almost no inflection in his voice.

He turned and went inside the house.

Kayla followed, pulling open the screen door and stepping into the cool dimness of the front hallway. She needed his help. She needed him to understand. She needed him, whether he liked it or not. "Look, Cal, I know I've caught you by surprise," she said quietly. "All I ask is that you hear me out."

Cal had gone into a cheerily decorated living room, the couch and easy chairs covered with blue gingham, bright paintings covering the walls. A huge window let in both the sunlight and a breathtaking view of the mountains. The room was large, with exposed beams and a huge fireplace at one end. He stood there now, hands braced against the heavy wooden mantel, staring at an array of framed pictures that lined its surface.

The pictures were of Liam. They, like the faded and worn gingham upholstery, were dated, relics from a happier time.

When Cal spoke, his voice was soft and still so oddly expressionless. "I loved him. Hell, I love him still. But he's dead."

"No, he's n—"

"Take my money," he said, louder now, turning to face her, a flare of sudden emotion lighting his eyes and heating his voice. "Take my truck. Take whatever the hell you want. Just don't make me believe something that can't possibly be true. If you're going to rob me blind, do it now and get it over with, but do it without tearing out my heart."

Kayla's own heart clenched. Dear God, if she were wrong, she would be torturing this man. But if she were right ... Even if the chance was only one in a thousand that she might be right, she had to take it. For Liam's sake.

"They told you he died in an explosion on a bus," she said. "Right?"

Cal dropped his head in a gesture of defeat. "Please, don't do this—"

"They told you countless witnesses saw him board that bus in the city of Puerto Norte," she continued. "But every single piece of your information came from the same source—the San Salustiano government officials, right?"

He didn't say a word. He just stood there, looking out at the mountains, his eyes once again flat, his face expressionless.

"Right?" she repeated, but still he didn't move. "I know, because I got the same explanations, the same official letters. But what if it's a cover-up? What if he didn't really die? What if he's being held hostage or prisoner? What if they only want us to believe that he's dead? He wasn't in San Salustiano to write a travelogue, you know. He was there to dig up dirt about the recent political and civil unrest. What if he found out something that their government didn't want the rest of the world to know?"

Calvin Bartlett turned and walked away.

She followed him into the kitchen. "His body was never recovered—"

He spoke matter-of-factly as he took a coffee mug down from the cabinet. "Because there was nothing of him left. Because he was blown to pieces."

"*Conveniently* blown to pieces. Or so they claimed."

Cal laughed, but it was a dry, humorless sound. He filled the mug of water from the tap and put it into a microwave oven.

"None of his jewelry was ever recovered," Kayla persisted. "His journalism award ring—what happened to it? He never took it off. If he really did get on that bus, then he was wearing that ring. So where did it go?"

He stared at his mug of water spinning round and round on the microwave's carousel as it heated. "It was probably fired out of that bus like a piece of shrapnel when that bomb went off."

"Unless he wasn't on that bus."

Cal turned and looked at Mikayla Grey. His brother's lover. The woman who had smiled at him and sighed with him all last night in his intensely erotic dreams. She was gazing at him so fiercely now. Her green eyes were blazing as if she were trying to burn her way into his brain to read his very thoughts.

She would have been shocked. Hell, *he* was shocked at the direction his mind continued to wander. He still wanted her. Badly.

She was wearing a pair of cutoff black jean shorts, with a clingy T-shirt made of some kind of sweater material on top. She had those funky black boots on her feet, and sure enough, Liam's enormous rodeo ring on a chain around her neck. Her face was pale, several distinct freckles standing out on her nose. Her eyes seemed too big for her face.

Maybe she was a con artist. Maybe she wasn't. Maybe she was just plain crazy. Either way, Liam had loved her. And here *he* was, unable to look at her without wanting to kiss her sweet lips again, without wanting to touch and taste the soft skin he knew was underneath that sweater and those shorts.

He hated himself for it, hated himself for being the brother who had survived.

"I work at a crisis center for abused women in Boston," Kayla told him softly, and he knew that somehow he was able to hide everything he was thinking and feeling. "I'd been working on my Spanish—it helps to be bilingual in a job like that. But you can't learn in a classroom the kind of Spanish I need to be able to speak, so I started going down to an inner-city church where there's a soup kitchen and a shelter. I figured I could help out *and* learn something at the same time."

She took a deep breath. "A lot of the people who came in were illegals, many of them refugees, some from San Salustiano. I heard some real horror stories about the war—you wouldn't believe what some of these people have been through. And then I started hearing about some kind of secret military prison hidden up in the mountains, where there was rumored to be a blond Americano being held against his will."

"Rumored."

Cal's voice was flat, implying disbelief, but Kayla felt a rush of relief. He was listening. At least he was listening.

She took a step toward him. "I couldn't stop thinking about it, and I went to see a woman who claimed she'd actually seen this man. I talked to her, Cal. And she described Liam so *exactly*. The way he walked. The way he laughed. And then I showed her a picture of Liam, and she said he was the one—the Americano."

"And she just happened to wander into some high security, top secret military prison and get a look at the prisoners?"

"She said she went inside to deliver clean laundry for her sister-in-law, who couldn't make the normal delivery run because her baby was sick. She said while she was there, they brought Liam out into the courtyard and ..." Her voice faltered. "They beat him."

There was only the faintest flicker of reaction in Cal's flinty eyes.

"She told me they tied him up and whipped him. She said it was clear that this wasn't the first time—his back was already raw and what wasn't raw was badly scarred." Kayla held Cal's gaze as she dropped her bomb. "She told me that the entire time they beat him, he sang Christmas carols. It was the beginning of the summer. It was a hundred degrees in the shade, and the blond-haired prisoner was singing Christmas songs."

Cal moved to the kitchen table and sat down, raking his thick hair back with one hand.

"He sang in English, and he sang in Spanish," she told him quietly. "The harder they hit him, the louder he sang. And she said when they untied him and dragged him back to his cell, he could barely walk, but he still held his head up high. She told me he saw her watching him and he smiled at her."

Cal looked up at her, directly into her eyes, and Kayla knew that she had won. He believed her. He believed that the man the San Salustiano woman had seen was his brother.

"How long ago did she see him there?" he asked, his voice rough.

"It was a little more than three months ago. The end of May."

He gripped the edge of the table. "My God."

She sat down across from him. "I know. It seems impossible, but . . . It's got to be him."

"Christmas carols . . ."

"I know. He sang them all the time. Any time of

year. It drove me nuts. He claimed they were the only songs he knew all the words to. It's *got* to be him."

"But he doesn't speak Spanish."

"I guess he's had the time to learn, because it sounds like he speaks it now."

"My *God*. Two *years*..." Cal shook his head. "He was never that strong. This woman who told you this story could be mistaken."

Kayla gazed at him levelly. "She could be. But I have to find out for sure. And if it really *is* Liam..."

If it really was Liam, she would find a way to free him and bring him home.

"I need your help," she told Cal Bartlett. "I want to go to San Salustiano, and I need you to come with me."

She would be safer traveling with a man. Kayla didn't like it, but knew it was true. She had spoken to workers at the San Salustiano consulate in New York City who had warned her that the political situation on the tiny island country was volcanic—with the threat of civil war continuously simmering beneath the surface. And despite the San Salustiano government's attempts to convince the world that all was well, and to restore the tourist trade, a woman—particularly an American woman traveling alone—would bring undue attention to herself.

She gazed across the table at Cal, waiting for him to say something, *any*thing.

"If you think Liam is still alive, then what the hell were you doing kissing me last night?"

Of all the things she'd expected him to say, that was not on the list.

But he was the one who kissed her first. The childish, blame-pointing words leapt to her tongue, but she kept her lips tightly shut. Yes, he'd certainly kissed her first, but she'd kissed him back with equal enthusiasm.

Her gaze dropped to the hard line of his mouth as she remembered how soft and sweet his lips had been. When she looked up into his eyes, she knew he'd clearly followed the direction of her thoughts.

"I don't know," she answered honestly. "You saved my life. You're different from anyone I've ever met. You look great in firelight. I don't *know*. I can come up with a hundred different excuses, but the truth is, I don't have an excuse."

Cal stood up, pushing his chair back from the table. "It never happened," he said. "As of right now, we don't talk about it, we don't *think* about it. Is that clear?"

Kayla had to look away from the icicle blueness of his eyes. She didn't like what he was saying, but she nodded. She needed his help, so she'd play by his rules. For now, anyway.

"Go on back to the boardinghouse, collect your things, and meet me back here," he ordered tersely. "We'll take my plane down into the city, catch a flight from there to San Salustiano."

He turned his back on her to dial the phone, and she stood there for a moment before realizing she'd been dismissed.

"Yeah," she heard him say in his soft western drawl as she let herself out the front door. "Flying out of Billings. Or Great Falls. It doesn't matter which. I need two seats on the next flight leaving for the Caribbean."

They were on their way.

This had to be the longest flight in the history of the world. Cal shifted in his seat, trying to find a comfortable position. His leg bumped Kayla's and she glanced up from the book she was reading.

"Sorry," he murmured.

She pushed up the armrest that separated them and pulled her legs up onto the seat, tailor-style. "Stretch your legs over this way," she told him, gesturing toward the open space in front of her seat.

He didn't want to do it. It would mean that her knee would rest tantalizingly on top of his thigh. But if he didn't do it, he wasn't going to be able to walk by the time this damned plane landed in the city of Puerto Norte.

He stretched out his legs. She settled back, her own leg lightly resting against his.

The place where she was touching him seemed to burn, and try as he might, he couldn't think about anything but the fact that they were sitting too damned close.

It never happened, he'd told her about those powerful kisses they'd shared just the night before. *As of right now, we don't talk about it, we don't think about it.*

Don't think about it. Right. He'd been able to think of little else from the moment he'd uttered those words.

His brother's lover, he silently told himself over and over again. Kayla Grey was his brother's lover.

"Liam used to talk about you all the time," she said softly, and he looked up to find her watching him. Her brownish-green eyes were so exactly the color of the hillside back behind his barn, he felt as if he were carrying a piece of home along with him.

"Funny," he said, "he never spoke to me about *you*."

She just smiled at his words. "You know, he mentioned you could be a real nasty bastard when provoked." She closed her book, putting the paper wrapping from a straw between the pages to mark her place. "Can we call a truce here?"

The muscles in his legs twinged, and he shifted in his seat again. "I thought we had."

"No," she said, slipping the book into the pouch attached to the seat in front of her before she turned to face him. "No, you barked out some

kind of command about how we were both supposed to ignore and deny the very human, very
natural , , *interaction* we shared last night."

Interaction? Damn right it was interaction.
And it had come dangerously close to a whole lot
more action.

"This...*attraction* between us isn't something
we have to be embarrassed about," she continued.
"We're grown-ups. We can deal with this without
having to pretend it didn't happen."

Cal resisted the urge to put his head back and
cover his face with his cowboy hat. He suspected if
he did, she'd keep talking to him anyway. No, he
would just sit there, silently, and let her talk herself out.

"You didn't know who I was," she persisted.

"But *you* knew who you were," he couldn't resist commenting, even though he'd vowed to stay
silent.

Kayla's graceful lips curled up into a very
small, faintly bitter smile. "My mistake was in
wanting to be held." She glanced up at him, her
eyes flashing. "If I remember correctly, I asked you
only to hold me. I didn't ask you to kiss me until
the room spun."

Until the room spun? Had the room really spun
for her too?

Their gazes caught and held, and for one brief,
molten moment, Cal was sure he was going to

reach for her again. For a fraction of a second he'd almost thought he had. But if he'd moved, he'd also stopped himself. God help him, he'd *better* stop himself.

"You shouldn't have let me kiss you," he countered harshly. "Lord knows I couldn't help myself, but you—"

"Oh, *please*," she scoffed. "Don't give me that 'I'm a man, I couldn't help myself, but you're a woman, it's your job to stop me' garbage. Too many men fail to take responsibility for themselves and their actions. Too many men cop out and blame testosterone for their own weakness."

"All right, it's all my fault—is that what you want to hear? I didn't know who you were. You were beautiful, you were barely dressed, you were all alone, and I wanted you." Damnation, he wanted her still. His desire was surely written clearly in his eyes, but he held her gaze anyway, daring her to acknowledge it.

"If you ask me to hold you again," he continued softly, "I won't make the same mistake. Because I *do* take responsibility for my actions. Because I *don't* cop out. And because I honor my brother's feelings—even if you don't."

"Last night was a highly emotionally charged situation for both of us," she whispered, color spreading across her delicate cheekbones.

And so was the situation they were heading

directly toward. It, too, was life and death, and just as fraught with emotional peril.

It had been nearly four months since Liam had last been seen. That is, assuming the American prisoner truly *was* Liam. If he was, four months was a long time for a man who was beaten and tortured regularly to stay alive....

Cal didn't want to let himself hope, but it was already too late. He *did* hope. Sweet Lord, he was beyond hoping. He was thinking in terms of when, not if. *When* they found the kid... *When* they figured out a way to get him out of the prison and off the island... *When* he brought Liam back to the ranch...

If he was wrong, if the kid had died in that bus explosion... He didn't want to think about it, didn't want to think what that would do to him.

He looked at Kayla. She was quiet now, but she hadn't picked up her book again. Her hands were clasped tightly in her lap, her knuckles nearly white from the pressure. Her eyes were brimming with tears that she refused to allow to escape. She blinked them valiantly back.

She loved Liam too.

The thought hit him hard in the gut and he knew his words to her had been too harsh, too cruel. She *did* love Liam. She'd come all the way to Montana to get the help she needed to search for him.

And now she was sitting there, with each passing moment a little bit closer to finding out if he was dead, as they'd been told, or still alive.

Maybe she didn't love Liam as well as she should have, but she *did* love him. This had to be as hard on her as it was on Cal. And his cruel intolerance was only making it worse.

"Where exactly did you meet Liam?" he asked softly, both wanting to know and wanting her to know that there could, indeed, be a truce between them. And not just for Liam's sake.

Fresh tears flooded her eyes, and he had to turn and pretend he didn't notice her wiping them away.

"In Boston," she told him. "He was writing an article on date rape and he came into the crisis center where I work. He wanted to do a 'day in the life of a crisis center worker' kind of sidebar for the piece, and he followed me around for twenty-four hours straight, writing down everything I said and did." She smiled softly at the memory, her eyes distant. "The article was wonderful. It sparked interest in the center that got us additional funding." She looked up at Cal. "He told me he always sent you copies of everything he wrote. Do you remember reading it? It was about eight months before he left for San Salustiano."

Cal nodded. He remembered. "I'll have to look

at it again. I don't remember your name being in there."

"It wasn't " She leaned her head back against the seat as she looked at him. "The names were all changed to protect the innocent."

"So that's when you ... became involved with him?"

Kayla shook her head no. "That's when we became friends. He was seeing someone and I ... I had my own agenda to work through. We didn't start dating until right before he—"

Died. She was going to say died.

"—right before he left for the Caribbean." She lifted the rodeo ring she was wearing on a chain around her neck, watching the light sparkle on the shiny red stone. "He asked me to marry him on our first official date. I still think his proposal was just an attempt to get me into bed."

What on earth had possessed her to say *that*? Kayla had to look away from the cowboy, afraid to see his reaction to her words reflected in his pale blue eyes. From now on she had to avoid all references to sex, no matter how vague. Because there was something there between them, something almost tangible, something powerful. Something much too dangerous to fool with.

"Hell of a ploy," Cal drawled, "considering he was willing to trade the rest of his life for the pleasure."

"Liam wasn't...very good at long-term planning," she said, choosing her words cautiously. "He didn't think much beyond the here and now. In fact, I'm not sure he gave much thought to the concept of marriage involving the rest of his life."

To her surprise, Cal chuckled. "I guess you *did* know him pretty well, didn't you?"

"Not as well as he wanted me to know him."

His eyes narrowed slightly in disbelief, and Kayla had to look away again, suddenly embarrassed at the intimate secrets her words had revealed.

She hadn't slept with Liam. She hadn't been ready to, not even after having known him for eight months. Yet she'd come impossibly close to making love to his brother, closer than she had come in years to making love to anyone, after only an hour-and-a-half-long acquaintance.

Kayla didn't want to think about what that might mean. She *wouldn't* think about it. She hadn't come this far to be distracted by a man who was such a curious and fascinating mix of soft and hard, hot and cold, gentle understanding and cruel intolerance.

"I spoke to as many people as I could about how to approach the San Salustiano government regarding Liam," she told the rancher. He was watching her closely, as if he were trying to probe her mind. It was disconcerting and intimidating, and she gazed back at him, trying not to let him see her squirm.

His faded cowboy hat was resting on one knee, and he'd run his fingers through his jet-black hair, leaving it tousled and tumbling forward across his forehead. His rugged face was weathered from the sun, with deep wrinkles etched alongside his odd-colored eyes. His eyes *should* have been the warmest shade of deep brown, not this zero-degree grayish-blue.

Kayla searched his face for any similarity to Liam. Cal's slightly hooked nose was different, as were his exotically wide cheekbones. Everything about him was different—the shape of his face, the color of his hair, the strength of his chin.

His mouth. There was something about his mouth that proclaimed the two men brothers. Maybe.

Kayla realized he was waiting for her to continue speaking, but she'd long since lost her train of thought. "Liam didn't—*doesn't*—look very much like you."

"We had different mothers."

Liam had told her that. Cal's mother was part Native American—from the Crow tribe, Liam had said. Her heritage was evident in Cal's height and darkly handsome face. She also knew that his mother had died when Cal was five. Both brothers had that in common—although Cal hadn't had an older brother to care for him.

But Liam hadn't told her that he and his older brother were as different as night and day. Liam was loquacious. He was charming and charismatic and sparkling with good humor. He was a relentless talker, filling any silences with stories and opinions and snatches of song.

Cal, on the other hand, didn't speak unless he absolutely had to. Even then he was terse and to the point.

Kayla gave him a tentative smile. "Your mother was the talkative one, right?"

She saw it. A flash of genuine amusement in his eyes. It was a smile, even though it didn't quite reach his lips.

"I figure if you know Liam as well as you claim to, considering the way the kid could talk, you know all there is to know about me."

Kayla *did* know quite a bit. She knew that Cal had dropped out of high school the day he turned sixteen in order to run the ranch and provide for his little brother. She knew that there were many relentless, grueling hours involved in being a working rancher. She knew he'd given Liam everything he'd ever asked for. She knew he'd held Liam's undying loyalty and deep-flowing brotherly love.

"I know only what Liam knew," she said. "I

think there's probably a whole lot more you never told him."

There was the faintest flicker in Cal's eyes, but he looked away before she could tell whether or not she had imagined it.

"You know about me, but I don't really know you at all," he said. "Where'd you grow up? Are you from Boston?"

"Boston suburbs," she said. "Let's see, my childhood in a nutshell: No sisters, one brother—older than me by five years, a dog named George—younger than me by five years. Dad worked in middle management at an insurance company in the city, and Mom stayed at home, did volunteer work at the church. I had a classic American sit-com upbringing—without the cheesy laugh track. Every episode had a happy ending. I graduated from high school and went to Boston University—English major, Spanish minor. I was going for my teaching degree."

He was watching her steadily, as if well aware that all of her information had been superficial. "But now you're a social worker. What made you switch from teaching?"

Kayla gazed back at him, wondering how vague she should make her reply. Something in his pale blue eyes dared her to tell him, *really* tell him something personal about herself, tell him who she was.

So she told him. Bluntly. No apologies, no gentle words of warning to soften the truth. "I was raped."

She could see disbelief flash into his eyes, followed quickly by the realization that she was dead serious. He didn't try to hide his shock and his horror, and he didn't look away in embarrassment the way some people did, as if her admission were something of which to be ashamed.

So she told him even more. "Sophomore year of college. I went out on a date with an upperclassman who didn't believe me when I said I didn't want to get it on with him." She took a deep breath. She had his total attention, so she went on. "It was date rape. At the time I didn't even know there was a name for it. I was too ashamed even to tell my roommate. It's amazing the things you think when something like this happens to you. You think, it must've been my fault, I must've done something wrong, I must've said something to make him think I wanted this.... It really messed me up. I wanted to climb into my bed and hide for the rest of my life.

"But I was hurt badly enough to need to go to the health center," she continued softly. "The doctor there knew I'd been raped, and she asked me if I wanted to notify the police and press charges. I said no. Who would believe me? The boy was incredibly popular. He was smart and rich and a great athlete. Girls were dying to go out with him.

God, I'd thought I was so lucky when he asked me to the movies." She laughed—a snort of disbelief loaded with twenty-twenty hindsight. "So I just . . . never told anyone. At least not for about a year. I spent that year hiding from the world."

For the first time since she'd started telling her story, Cal shifted in his seat. "You don't strike me as the kind of woman who hides from her problems."

"You'd be amazed what something like rape can do to even the strongest of women."

"What happened?" he asked softly. "What helped you learn to deal with it?"

Kayla gazed into this man's eyes, and found herself telling him something she'd never admitted to anyone. "In some ways I can't deal with it," she said. "In some ways I don't know if I'll *ever* be able to deal with it." Like when it came to making love, to sharing intimacies. "I have managed to convince myself that what happened to me was not my fault though, that what that boy did was *wrong*. And that's a solid start."

She looked away from him, suddenly terribly self-conscious. "So now you probably know a whole lot more about me than you wanted to know, huh?"

"I still want to know how you got hooked up with the Boston Women's Crisis Center," he said quietly.

"About a year later, the man who'd raped me

was arrested," she said. "Another girl pressed charges, and they went to trial. The Boston Women's Crisis Center helped her post flyers— looking for other women who might've been assaulted by the same guy, to help with her case against him. I saw the flyer and called the hotline number. The woman I spoke to talked me into coming down to the center for a visit." She glanced up at him. "I can't tell you how incredible it was to talk to women who'd been right where I was. It was such a relief to be allowed to be angry and finally to acknowledge the fact that when that boy raped me, I wasn't simply getting what I deserved." She paused. "I wanted to help other women the way the center workers helped me. So I switched my major, did an extra year of study in social work and . . . here I am."

Cal was silent for a moment, turning his hat around in his hands. And when he spoke, his words surprised her. "Last night . . ." He met her eyes. "I hope I didn't frighten you."

He was talking about when he'd kissed her.

"If I did, I'm truly sorry," he continued.

"There was no way you could have known," she said. "And besides, you didn't. Frighten me." On the contrary—she'd frightened herself. He was the first man in an eternity that she'd even halfway considered becoming intimate with. The thought still unnerved her enough to consciously change the subject. "We should talk about the best way to try to locate Liam."

Cal shifted again. "You got something in mind besides just asking questions?"

"The people I spoke to thought it might be best if we don't announce our arrival in Puerto Norte," Kayla told him. "They thought we should pretend to be tourists and take a look around before we contact any officials. If the government *is* hiding Liam, we don't want them to bury him so deep that we'll never find him."

He was silent, still turning his hat around and around and around.

"We should wait," she added, "and go through official channels only if we don't find out anything any other way—if we need to shake things up."

He nodded slowly, glancing at her, and she knew he was thinking the same thing she was. Their presence in San Salustiano could very well put Liam in even more danger.

"So we're tourists," he said, his eyes suddenly as cold and as grim as the thin line of his lips, "coming to a war-torn island for a fun-filled vacation. Who the hell is going to believe *that*?"

Cal watched Kayla smile sunnily at the customs official as the dour-faced man perused both of their passports.

Despite what he'd thought, there was a surprising number of vacationers going through customs. But despite the country's desire for a brisker tourist trade, the customs officials were unfriendly, and escorted several people to a private room for a thorough body search.

Cal didn't want that to happen. He was carrying copies of the documents he'd received from the San Salustiano government concerning Liam's death. His alleged death. But if he and Kayla were going to pretend to be tourists and not tip anyone off as to the real reason they'd come to the island, it was important those papers weren't uncovered in a strip search.

He didn't know what papers Kayla had hidden under her lightweight jacket, but he suspected she was carrying something equally incriminating.

"We don't want to be strip-searched," he breathed into her ear. She nodded, her smile never faltering. God, after what she'd told him on the plane, she may not have wanted to be strip-searched for an entirely different reason.

The customs official said something to them in Spanish, and Kayla replied, rapid fire, going on and on and on—about what, Cal didn't know. She stopped just as quickly as she'd started and smiled up at Cal, slipping her arm around his waist.

The shock of the sudden full body contact was nearly overwhelming, and he started to pull away—until she pinched him, just above the waistband of his jeans, her hand hidden underneath his jacket.

"Act like you like me, for God's sake," she hissed through still-smiling teeth. "Pretend that you want me."

Pretend that he wanted her.

Cal was a lousy actor, but this was something he could handle. Because despite all his attempts to convince himself otherwise, he *did* want her.

He pulled her in front of him, encircling her with his arms, letting his hands wander the curve of her hips, across and up her taut stomach, his thumbs brushing the soft undersides of her breasts. Her derriere was pressed against him, and he pulled her even closer as he nuzzled her neck. Sweet God, she smelled good and tasted even better.

"What did you tell him?" he breathed into Kayla's ear.

She turned to face him, slipping her arms up around his neck, and the sensation of her breasts pressed against his chest was nearly too much to handle.

"I said we'd come here because this was the last place my father would think to look for us," she whispered breathlessly. "I said you'd talked me into running away with you, and that even though you had a terrible reputation as a Don Juan, I was certain you were going to propose marriage any minute."

She stood on tiptoe to kiss him, pulling his head down until his lips met hers.

He shouldn't be kissing her—for more than one reason, not the least of which was that story she'd told him on the plane. But he had to help her fool the customs official into thinking they were harmless vacationers. He *had* to kiss her, whether or not either of them wanted to.

But God knows he *did* want to kiss her. And this could very well be the last time he'd ever have such a good excuse. He deepened their kiss, gently claiming the soft sweetness of her mouth with his tongue, carefully holding back, careful not to overpower her, all the while wishing with quiet desperation that he could indeed be some kind of ruthless Don Juan, uncaring of little besides his own selfish needs.

Kayla was trembling when he released her, and to his surprise, he saw a reflection of his own guilty pleasure in her eyes.

It was better than seeing fear and revulsion, but not by much.

He glanced over at the customs official. The man was watching them with unabashed interest, and Cal smiled and gave him a slow wink as he let his hands stray over the soft curve of Kayla's rear end, pulling her closer one more time.

The man winked back and stamped the passports, waving them away from the uniformed men and women handling the more detailed body searches and toward the airport door.

Arm in arm they headed toward the taxi stand, one small step closer to finding Liam.

— 6 —

Kayla went into Cal's hotel room through the balcony. "These rooms are enormous. They must've given us two of their royal suites. I guess despite their advertising campaign, the tourist trade is still way down these days. This entire hotel is only a quarter full."

Cal was standing in the middle of the opulent room, and he turned to face her as she came in.

"We need to rent a car," she said briskly, thinking aloud, "and go up into the m—"

"The first thing we need to do," Cal interrupted, "is try out that big old king-sized bed over there on the other side of the room."

Kayla took an involuntary step backward as he moved toward her, an unmistakable glint in his eye. "But—"

He tossed his cowboy hat onto the desk and pulled his T-shirt over his head. "I've been waiting to get you alone for weeks," he said.

Weeks? But he'd known her only a matter of days. *Hours.*

He tossed his shirt so that it draped over the top of the television. He moved even closer to her, and this time Kayla couldn't move, mesmerized by the sight of his smooth, tanned skin. She was unable to block the memory of the night he'd saved her from the storm—the night he'd kissed her and she'd run her hands across the muscular expanse of his back and . . .

"And now that your daddy's not around to stop us . . ." he said, looking hard into her eyes.

Instantly, she knew that Cal hadn't gone stark raving mad. For some reason, he was playing along with the story she'd given the customs official at the airport. But why? They were alone in the room.

Or were they?

He glanced toward the desk, and following his gaze, she saw that he'd taken a writing pad out from the drawer. It lay on top, the words "Room bugged—video camera built into TV set" written clearly in his big, bold handwriting.

They were being watched. How had he known to look for a camera?

Cal put his arms around her waist, pulling her close, pressing her hips against his, bending down to catch her lips in a kiss that made her blood pound through her veins. It was a kiss that meant business, and her arms went up around him as if of their own accord. His bare skin was as satiny smooth as she remembered.

He tugged her own shirt free from her shorts, his callused fingers rough against her skin as he kissed her again. It was a kiss meant to look passionate, but his lips were gentle, his mouth impossibly sweet. It was a kiss meant to convince the people watching through the camera lens that had been cleverly hidden in the ornate façade of the big television. And it *would* convince them that she and Cal had only one thing on their minds—it very nearly had Kayla herself convinced.

And as for Cal... She could feel how much he was holding back. But she could also feel his arousal. She could taste his need.

She felt his hands travel up her back, underneath her shirt, felt his fingers touch the back strap of her bra as if checking to be sure that she even had one on.

"I'm going to take off your shirt, okay?" he breathed into her ear.

Take off her...?

He gently pulled her shirt up. "Come on, Kayla," he coaxed, louder now, her name sounding like music in his soft western drawl.

He must have had a reason for wanting to take her shirt off, but Kayla couldn't for the life of her figure out what that reason was. Was he intending to make love to her purely for the benefit of the camera? Would he do such a thing?

Would *she*?

She gazed up into the blue and gray swirl of his eyes as he tugged at her shirt again, needing her help to get it off her arms, over her head. A familiar surge of fear shot through her. "Cal, no—"

"It's okay," he murmured as if he were gentling a horse. He kissed her lips again, leaving a trail of kisses across her face until his mouth was only a whisper away from her ear. "Just your shirt," he breathed almost silently. "I need it to cover the camera lens."

He pulled back slightly, looking into her eyes questioningly, and she nodded. Yes. She lifted her arms, helping him pull her shirt up and over her head.

Her bra was black stretch lace and nearly transparent. She heard Cal draw in a quick breath, his eyes flashing with a heat that was all too real as he looked down at her.

He quickly turned away, throwing her shirt next to his on top of the TV. It hung down, over the control panel, and Kayla knew his seemingly casual toss had been well planned and well aimed.

"Is there only one?" she asked, and he sharply shook his head, holding one finger up in front of his mouth.

"I don't know who you've been with before,

darlin', but one's all I've got—and one's all I need,"
he said loudly, quickly crossing to the notepad and
pen. "Go ahead and touch it. It won't bite you."

What? Was he talking about...?

In his bold block writing he quickly printed a
message on the notepad.

"Microphone or listening device somewhere in
this room," Kayla silently read. "Keep talking
while we search."

He wanted her to make noise, Kayla realized.
He wanted her to help him fool whoever was listening into thinking that she and Cal were, indeed,
making love.

"Oh, *yeah*," he said, crossing the room and
opening the zipper of his leather bag. "Oh, baby, it
feels *good* when you touch me like that."

He took a clean T-shirt from his bag and tossed
it to Kayla, who quickly pulled it on.

"Oh, yeah," Cal continued as he began to
search the desk and the dresser for a hidden microphone. "Oh, yeah, don't stop what you're
doing...."

His voice was velvet. It was pure, smoking sex-
uality, and Kayla felt heat pool in her stomach and
start to spread throughout her entire body. The
muscles in his back and arms flexed as he lowered
himself to the floor to search underneath the desk.

He was gorgeous as sin—every last muscular
inch of him. He was gorgeous, and his words were

outrageously sexy, yet his words and his actions were thoroughly incongruous. He wasn't anywhere near her, and she was equally far away from him. The entire situation seemed utterly absurd.

"Oh, darlin', ever since I first set eyes on you," he murmured, "I had a fantasy about what that mouth of yours could do to me...."

Kayla clapped her hand over that very same mouth to keep from laughing aloud. A tiny strangled squeak escaped, and Cal glared up at her from his position on the floor, where he was looking underneath the desk. "Come on," he silently mouthed. "Help me."

Despite his glare, he couldn't hide the glint of amusement in his eyes. It curled the corners of his mouth, softening the harsh plane of his face, making him look younger but no less dangerous.

"Ooooh," Kayla moaned as she began searching the wall near the front door. "Oh, baby!"

From across the room Cal snorted with laughter, turning it quickly into a very authentic-sounding groan of pleasure.

There was nothing on the wall or the door frame, nothing along the baseboard. Of course, she wouldn't know what she was looking for if it came up and bit her in the butt.

"Oh, Cal, Cal, *Cal*!" She lifted the spread of the bed, looking underneath. The floor was smooth Mexican tile, and the bottom of the box spring was covered with a piece of fabric. If a microphone were hidden in there, they'd never find it without taking a knife to it.

But . . . if the microphone were hidden in there, then whoever was listening was about to get an earful.

Kayla jumped on top of the bed, bouncing it up and down, up and down. "Oh, yes!" she cried. "Yes! Don't stop!"

She couldn't keep from grinning at Cal as he swiftly moved across the room to search the bed-side table. To her surprise, he actually returned her smile, even giving her a glimpse of very white teeth as he went past.

She kept jumping on the bed as she turned to watch him examine the small cabinet. The top and sides were smoothly finished wood. An old-fashioned rotary-style telephone sat on top. Cal quietly and carefully lifted the phone to look underneath. Nothing.

"More!" Kayla cried. "Oooooh, Cal!"

He silently slid open the single drawer and looked inside. Nothing. At least not on the inside of the drawer.

Cal pulled the drawer the rest of the way out and peered up into the frame. He shifted position, lying on his back on the floor to get a better look. Then he sat back up, looking sharply up at Kayla, nodding and pointing to the darkness inside the bedside table. They found it. Someone was definitely listening.

Cal pulled himself to his feet in one smooth motion. She watched as he picked up the notepad and pen and wrote her another message. He handed the pad up to her.

"If we got a radio, and placed it near the mike, the music would mask our voices so that we could talk without being overheard," he had written.

She gestured for him to hand her the pen. "Why not just smash it?" she wrote.

Her handwriting was barely legible, but somehow he understood and wrote a reply.

"Then they'll know we know—and they'll just replace it with another, hidden somewhere else. We'd have to search the room again."

She held out her hand for the pen again. "How did you even know to look?"

"I read a lot," he wrote back. "I've read everything published on San Salustiano since Liam died. The government likes using electronic surveillance. Knowing that, along with the hotel bumping us up into these fancy rooms..."

He winced slightly, shaking a cramp out of his hand as he handed her the notepad. This was obviously an inefficient way of communicating. They needed to get a radio so they could talk.

"Cal," she moaned. "Oh, Cal, Cal, *wait*!" She

stopped her jumping, flopping down on the bed, gesturing wildly at him to respond.

"Darlin'," he said, not quite following her train of thought, but doing his best to keep up anyway. "Darlin', darlin'—what's wrong?"

"Music," Kayla said. "I can't...I simply can't make love without music."

The look on Cal's face was so incredible, Kayla lost it. She had to turn and bury her face into a pillow to keep her giddy laughter from being overheard.

"You want me to turn on the TV?" Cal's voice sounded very, very strange as he, too, fought to keep from laughing. He now knew exactly where she was heading.

She peeked out at him. "The TV's not very romantic," she somehow managed to say. "Besides, I don't think it would be loud enough. I like my music *loud*."

"How about we get us a radio?"

Kayla made her voice syrupy sweet. "Oh, Cal, honey, would you do that for me? Now? I mean, *right* now?"

"Right *now*...?!" He made his voice crack with sheer disbelief. It was perfect, and funny as hell. She hadn't realized he'd had much of a sense of humor before this.

He grinned at her, trying desperately to contain his own laughter. Hardly able to breathe, Kayla hit him with her pillow. He grabbed her, pinning her back against the bed and...

She saw it happen. One moment he was smiling at her, his eyes warm with laughter, his leg thrown across hers, his hands holding her hands up above her head. But the very next moment realization had struck. Just like that, the warmth and the laughter were gone, leaving behind only the molten heat of his very real desire. And just as quickly as the desire appeared, it was followed by shame.

He pulled himself off her quickly, as if he were burned by her touch.

"Let's ... get dressed and ... go into town. Try to find you a radio." He turned and vanished into the bathroom, leaving her alone.

"What do you think?" Cal asked, pushing the brim of his cowboy hat back on his head.

Kayla stared at him. "You want me to *ride* that thing?" she asked incredulously, turning to gaze at the rickety-looking old motorcycle. "Don't they have anything real? Maybe something with *four* wheels instead of one and a half ...?"

"Aw, Kayla, you're disappointing me," Cal drawled, the edge of his mouth curling up into what for anyone else would have been no change of expression, but for him was a major smile. "I thought a city girl like you would be into riding a bike."

Claiming to be hot and sticky from their flight, Kayla had showered and changed while he'd gone in search of transportation. She stood before him now, dressed in an extremely short black skirt and a snugly fitting white T-shirt. She wore her same funky black boots on her feet and a pair of equally funky oval-shaped purple sunglasses on her nose. Her hair was still slightly damp from her shower.

"So where're the helmets?" she asked, crossing her arms in front of her chest.

"It didn't come with any helmets."

She looked at him over the top of her sunglasses. "Excuse me? You let some con artist rent you a...a...death trap of a motorcycle without getting any helmets?"

Cal had to smile. He didn't know what it was about this girl, but when he was with her, he usually ended up smiling. Or madder than hell.

"Okay," he said. "Our first stop will be back at the rental shop to pick up a helmet."

"Yours will have to be a very interesting shape if you intend to wear that cowboy hat underneath it."

"I don't need a helmet."

"Yes, you do."

"This bike probably doesn't go fast enough to—"

Kayla stepped closer to him, lowering her voice and talking fast. "I didn't haul your ass all the way down here from Montana just to watch you die of a head injury sustained in a fall from some poor excuse for a motorcycle!"

"You didn't haul my ass anywhere, darlin'," he countered, giving her a look designed to wither very large, very tough cowboys. "I'm an experienced rider. There're no helmet laws down here, so whether or not I wear one is my choice. *My* choice."

Kayla didn't wither. She just looked at him. "Please," she finally said. "I forgot to say please. Will you *please* wear a helmet? For Liam's sake, if not mine. If he's here, if he's still alive, I'm going to need you in one piece to help me get him off this island."

The kid. She *had* to bring up the kid.

"Please?" she said again, reaching out to touch his arm.

Her touch burned him, as it always did, and he shook her off, swearing softly.

"Was that a yes dammit or a no dammit?"

"Yes, dammit."

"Thank you."

"Can we go now?"

Kayla took a deep breath, drawing his attention to her clinging T-shirt and the curves underneath it. "All right," she said, approaching the motorcycle. "Time for a motorcycle riding lesson." She turned back to look at him. "Where's *your* bike?"

Cal snorted. "Very funny. Hang on a sec—let me give my hat to one of the bellboys, to leave at the front desk." He took the marble stairs to the front doors of the elegant hotel three at a time and handed his Stetson to an impossibly young boy wearing a bell captain's uniform. "Front desk, please," he said, giving his room number in both English and Spanish, and the boy scurried off.

He came down the stairs more slowly, watching Kayla as she swung her leg over the worn padding of the motorcycle seat. He was wrong about what she was wearing. It wasn't a skirt—it was a very loose pair of shorts. Either way, it was incredibly sexy. A breeze blew, ruffling her short blond curls and lifting the bottom of her shorts, pushing them farther up her leg.

Damnation, he was in trouble here. What Cal was feeling, what he wanted, was *wrong*. But he couldn't get away from it. From the moment he'd laid eyes on Kayla, he'd wanted her. From the moment that she'd opened her eyes and looked up at him, from the moment she'd stood up in that tub like the grand prize winner of a wet T-shirt contest, from the moment he'd helped her out of her clothes, he'd been walking around in a constant state of arousal. He burned for this girl.

Kayla glanced at him, and Cal shook his head, trying to clear it of all thoughts but the ones that mattered: finding Liam.

"It's easier if you let me get on first," he told her.

She pulled off her sunglasses and gazed up at him in surprise. "We're riding this thing *together*?"

Cal nodded. "That's right. All you have to do is hold on."

She didn't move. "This means I'm going to have to touch you," she said bluntly. "You don't like it when I touch you."

He shook his head. "No, ma'am," he said. "I like it too much when you touch me."

Kayla didn't look away. She held his gaze, and the sweet sadness she let him see in her eyes was more intimate than a kiss. "This is a problem, isn't it?" she asked softly. "This thing—whatever it is—between us."

"Only if we let it be." He held on to the hand-grips of the motorcycle, gesturing with his head for her to hop off. She did, and he swung his leg over the seat, sitting far enough forward for her to fit behind him. She climbed on, and he had to close his eyes at the sensation of her legs pressed against him. He didn't dare look. The sight of her long, tanned legs against his jeans would have done him in. When he spoke again, his voice was raspy. "I for one don't intend to let it be. The way I see it, we've got more than enough to focus on with finding Liam and figuring out how to get him the hell out of here."

"It's just ..." Kayla spoke softly, but sitting behind him, her mouth was close to his ear. "It's chemistry, and it's not something either one of us asked for, so don't waste your time beating yourself up about it, all right? It's not your fault—I feel it too, you know."

God, was that supposed to make him feel better, knowing that this heat that threatened to consume him was something that she felt too? Was knowing that she, too, had to fight this relentless desire supposed to *help*? Was knowing that if he slipped, if he succumbed in a moment of weakness, she might not be able to stand firm, that she might be equally seduced by her own desires—was that supposed to give him confidence?

Cal started the motorcycle with a roar, silently cursing both Kayla and himself. Mostly himself.

"Careful where you put your legs," he warned her, shouting over the sudden noise. "The exhaust pipe gets hot."

He felt her arms go around his waist, felt her body press up against his back, and he had to wonder. Was this why he'd settled for renting this motorcycle? Was this why he hadn't searched harder for an establishment that could rent him a car? Had he intentionally given in too soon simply out of his need to feel Kayla's arms around him again?

"Please don't go too fast," she said into his ear.

He wanted to race. He wanted to push this piece of junk as fast as it could possibly go and feel the wind in his face and the rush of the pavement under his tires. He wanted to run away from himself and from Kayla and even from Liam.

Instead, he eased out into the road that led toward town, attaching an addendum to his constant prayers that they find the kid alive, asking the good Lord to expedite his request, to work overtime and help them find Liam *soon*.

"Are you crazy?" Kayla gazed at the elderly San Salustiano shopkeeper, well aware of Cal watching the exchange as she spoke in Spanish. "If you think we're going to pay seventy-five dollars American for that little piece of garbage, you're in for a disappointment."

"I can get more than one hundred dollars for this." The merchant sniffed. "I was giving you a discount because you are such a pretty young girl."

She picked up the cheap battery-operated radio. She flipped on the switch, and tinny, distorted salsa music blared from the inexpensive speaker. She quickly turned it off. "It's not even new. The knob is missing and the speaker is dented."

"This *is* a pawn shop. Nothing here is new."

"I'll give you twenty-five. Not a penny more."

The old man smiled, and Kayla knew that at one time he had broken more than his share of hearts. "Seventy. Not a penny less."

Cal put a small but deadly-looking knife in a plain leather holster on the counter. "Just pay him what he wants for both the radio and the knife, and let's get the hell out of here," he said.

Kayla ignored him. If he had read everything that had been written about San Salustiano, then he surely knew that this was the way things were bought and sold on the island. If she paid this man the inflated amount, he would be disappointed in her. He certainly wouldn't respect her, and he'd hesitate to give them any information he might have about the current political situation and the rumored prison camps in the mountains. Besides, as it was, the price she was prepared to settle on was ten times higher than the value of the radio. "Thirty. For both the radio *and* the knife."

"Both?" The shop owner rolled his eyes, turning to glance at the sweet-faced middle-aged woman who was behind the counter with him. Kayla couldn't tell if she was his daughter or his wife. "Sixty-five."

"Thirty-five."

"Sixty."

"Forty."

"Fifty-five."

"Forty." Kayla took two crisp twenty-dollar bills from her pocket, unfolding them and letting the shopkeeper have a look at Andrew Jackson's face. "Cash."

"Sold." He held out his hand and she slapped the money into it, then tossed the radio to Cal. She let him pick up the knife himself.

"Didn't I read somewhere that a recent San Salustiano law makes it illegal for merchants to accept American dollars?" he drawled.

The storekeeper hesitated only slightly as he rearranged his display of radios and telephones, and Kayla suspected the man knew more English than he had originally let on. In case she was wrong, she translated Cal's words into the man's native language.

"Many things are illegal in Puerto Norte these days," the old man quietly replied. "Things such as thinking, for example. It's no longer legal to have your own opinion in San Salustiano."

Kayla translated his words for Cal as the woman clucked worriedly. "Davio, don't speak of such things to strangers," she murmured.

Cal held Kayla's gaze, his eyes silently questioning. She knew what he was thinking. Did they dare to ask questions about Liam? She nodded slightly. They had to start somewhere.

"Ask him if he knows about the prison camps in the mountains," Cal told her. "Ask him if he's heard about Liam."

"I have heard talk," the old man said in only slightly accented English, "about such camps, though I've never seen them myself. Which is just as good, since I have heard that one doesn't see them until one is brought there as a prisoner. And once inside, there is no way out."

"You will have us all taken there, old man," the woman growled. With one last desperate look at Cal and Kayla, she left the room, disappearing behind a curtain.

"We're here looking for an American who disappeared two years ago," Kayla told the shopkeeper. "His name is William Bartlett—he was a news reporter from Boston. We've heard rumors from people who have left the island about a blond Americano held in one of the prison camps in the mountains—"

The old man was shaking his head. "I have heard of him too, and he is just a myth. Just a bogeyman to scare the villagers. The way the story goes, he escaped from one of the prison camps, badly injured, and was taken in by a family in a small village. They nursed him back to health and helped him find a boat to take him off the island. But somewhere along the way, they were betrayed. Government soldiers went into the village, but the Americano was nowhere to be found. In retaliation, the entire village was wiped out." He gazed levelly from Kayla to Cal. "It is no more than a fairy tale designed to frighten the 'children' of San Salustiano into behaving."

"I've talked to someone who saw the Americano," Kayla told the old man. "He *is* real."

He just smiled. "People see what they want to see. And these days, people want to see heroes."

"He always wore a gold journalism award ring on his right hand." Cal spoke up. "You haven't seen something like that come into this shop, have you?"

"No, sir." The man shook his head. "I have not heard of such a ring among my competitors either—and they would not have hesitated to brag if it was indeed real gold. If I hear anything, I will let you know."

"We're staying at the resort."

The old man nodded, then turned away, disappearing into the back room.

Kayla followed Cal out of the gloom of the shop and into the bright sunlight of the afternoon.

"Do you trust him?" she asked quietly.

"Right now I don't think I trust anyone," he replied, unlatching the small bag that was attached to the back of the motorcycle seat. He put the radio inside and closed it securely. Where he had put the knife Kayla didn't know—and she wasn't sure she wanted to know.

"Don't look now," he added quietly, "but there's a car on the corner that's following us. I saw it before, when I was out picking up the bike."

Kayla looked everywhere but at the corner.

From her peripheral vision she could see the car. It was black and sleek and more expensive than all of the rest of the cars on the street combined.

"I saw it before too," she said. "It was at the resort when we first arrived."

Cal climbed onto the motorcycle as she took her helmet off the handlebars and strapped it under her chin. "Want to see if whoever it is keeps following us?"

"Yeah. Where to?"

"Someplace crowded."

"The beach?"

Cal nodded, starting the bike with a roar. She climbed on behind, holding tightly to him, trying not to notice how good he smelled or how solid and powerful his muscles felt beneath her arms.

He drove slowly through town, gradually picking up speed as he pulled onto a narrow road that seemed to cut directly through the tropical jungle.

"Where are we going?" Kayla shouted over his shoulder and into his ear.

"Like you said—to the beach."

Sure enough, she could see turquoise water sparkling through the thick underbrush. The road wound down the hillside, opening up into a nearly full parking lot. Cal slowed the bike, pulling right to the edge of the beach.

It was beautiful. The sand was blindingly white, and the ocean and the sky were in fierce competition for the world's most striking shade of blue. The two-mile-long beach was at the inside curve of a large U-shaped cove, beyond which the ocean stretched on and on, seemingly forever.

"He didn't follow us," Kayla said. The black car still hadn't pulled into the parking lot.

"He didn't need to follow us right away," Cal told her. "According to the map, that road we were on deadends here at the beach. As soon as we took that right turn, he knew exactly where we were going. My bet is he'll show up soon enough."

He waited for her to climb off the bike, then swung his leg over the seat. He took off his helmet and stood staring out at the water.

Underneath her helmet Kayla's curls were damp with perspiration. She ran her fingers through her hair, hooking the strap of the helmet on the back of the motorcycle. She kicked off her boots and wiggled her toes in the warm sand. "Aren't you going to take off your boots?"

"Yeah." Cal sat down in the sand and pulled off his cowboy boots and peeled off his socks. His shirt followed soon after. It was funny. Even with his shirt off and his jeans rolled up, he still looked like a cowboy, at home on the range, but out of place on the beach.

"Come on, let's walk." He set off toward the water, his stride so long, Kayla nearly had to trot to keep up with him. But he stopped at the edge of the ocean, letting the warm water wash over his feet, just gazing out at the shimmering blueness.

"Living in Montana, you probably don't have the opportunity to go to the beach very often," Kayla realized aloud.

He glanced at her. "About four years ago I flew to Boston and spent a week on Cape Cod with Liam. It was the first time I ever saw the ocean." His face softened into a small smile. "Needless to say, I was impressed."

"I grew up near the water," she told him. "I can't imagine the impact of seeing it for the first time as an adult."

"It's . . . pretty damn scary."

Kayla smiled. "I never would've expected you to admit that—not in a million years. That's good—I think the ocean deserves to be treated with healthy respect."

"Healthy respect? I'm not the world's strongest swimmer—now, *there's* an understatement—and the damn thing damn near scared me to death. Look at it out there, always moving, like some giant, beautiful, awful living thing, waiting to take some poor, unsuspecting fool and pull him under. Hell, what I've got is a genuine, full-blown, almost-out-of-control, wet-my-pants fear of the ocean. With a capital F."

She had to laugh. "I can't believe it. The way

Liam talked about you, you were fearless and invincible. Superman's first cousin."

The ocean breeze lifted his hair, pushing it forward into his face, then sweeping it out of his eyes as he started to walk along the edge of the water. "The kid didn't have a clue about a lot of things. But I guess I misled him on purpose, starting back when he was little. He'd already lost enough when his mama and daddy died, so I figured I had to make him believe I could take care of him no matter what. I couldn't let him know how close we came almost every year to losing the ranch. Lord, those first few years were tough. And when he got older . . . it's hard just to turn around and start confessing that you've spent most of your life scared witless about something as foolish as money."

"He told me he wasn't sure exactly what you were worth, but he thought you were extremely well off. He said that anytime he needed money during college, you sent it to him right away. No problem."

"No problem. That's a good one." Cal squinted slightly as he gazed out at the horizon. "I found . . . *creative* ways to get him money for school. But they were rarely problem-free."

"Such as?"

He bent down to pick up a shiny piece of sea glass, rubbing its smooth surface with his thumb. He glanced up at her, and she could see indecision in his eyes. This was far more personal even than admitting he was afraid of the water. She knew this was something he hadn't ever talked about. Not with Liam. Not with anyone.

She nudged him with her toe. "Come on, Bartlett. You've got me curious now. Did you rob a bank to pay for Liam's Harvard education? Or—I know—you posed nude for one of those women's magazines, right? Wearing only your boots and your hat?"

He laughed at that, tossing the sea glass back into the water and straightening up. "I never considered *that* option. Robbing a bank I maybe thought about for seven whole seconds..."

"So what *did* you do?"

"I made investments, played the stock market. Although that didn't always work." He brushed the sand off his hands on the thighs of his jeans. "Right before the second semester payments were due for Liam's junior year, the market took a nose-dive and I lost damn near everything. I had two thousand dollars in my savings account, and I needed a whole hell of a lot more than that to pay the kid's college bill, so...I got in my truck and drove down to Las Vegas." He glanced at her, and she saw that now-familiar glint of humor in his eyes once more. They started walking again. "I got the money, but I swear, I aged ten years in two and a half days."

"You don't seem like a gambler to me."

"I'm not." He smiled, but it was rueful. "And there's the irony. My entire life has been one long-shot gamble after another. Running a ranch is no sure thing. If disease doesn't get you, the weather will. If it's not a drought, it's a flood. The only guarantee you've got is that you'll work seven days a week, sunup to sundown, and sometimes even longer." He broke off, shaking his head. "I don't mean to sound as if I'm complaining, because I'm not. The past five years or so have been good. Financially, that is." He made a sound that came out more like a sob than a laugh. "I'm finally set, and Liam's not around to share it. God, I'd give it all back if only I could find him and bring him home. If he's still alive, I swear, I'll be content for the rest of my days."

It might have been the slight catch in his voice, or it might have been the sheer desperation in his eyes. Whichever it was, it drew Kayla to him. Before he could back away, she put her arms around him, offering comfort. He hesitated only a second before he took what she offered, and more. He pulled her close, burying his face in her hair, squeezing her so tightly, she could barely breathe.

Cal couldn't move. He had Kayla in his arms, pressed close enough for her to know without a doubt that he wanted her, and still he couldn't move. His desire rose up so swiftly, it shocked him. But he knew his desire was no more than just that—just a physical yearning He had to control himself He had to keep his priorities straight. He had to find Liam and bring him safely home. But even knowing that, Cal couldn't back away. He clung to Kayla almost desperately, knowing it was wrong to want her this way, but powerless to stop.

"It's going to be all right," Kayla murmured. Her hands were in his hair, on his neck, down his back, stroking, soothing, as if he were a child needing reassurance.

What he needed was for her to get far, *far* away from him. But still he couldn't move.

She lifted her head, looking up at him. "We'll find him," she said.

Her mouth was mere inches away from his. All he had to do was to lower his head . . .

"It's just a matter of time now," she continued. He moved closer. . . .

"Tomorrow we can take a ride up into the mountains and . . ." Her words trailed off, and he saw recognition in her eyes. Recognition and something else. She knew that he wanted to kiss her, and for a moment it looked as if she wanted that too.

The look in her eyes nearly pushed him over the edge. But for over twenty years, Cal had denied himself selfish and short-term pleasures, and he'd be damned if his self-control was going to be shattered now, when Liam needed him most, and when Kayla, too, desperately needed him not to push too hard.

Slowly, jerkily, Cal somehow managed to release her. Somehow he stepped back, away from her. He ran his hand through his hair, shocked not that it was shaking, but that it wasn't shaking *more*.

He'd done it. He'd managed not to kiss her.

This time.

Next time he wasn't sure he'd be able to stop himself.

He cleared his throat. "First thing in the morning I want to ride up into the mountains—try to find that prison camp."

Kayla cleared her throat too. She wasn't sure what had just happened. Cal had held her so tightly, she'd felt his heart racing, felt his pulse pounding. And now, here he was, pretending again that whatever it was between them was something that could be ignored. "All right. What time do you want me to be ready to leave?"

He glanced at her. "I was thinking I'd go alone."

"Without me?"

"That's generally what alone means. Without anyone else."

He turned to start walking down the beach, but she moved in front of him, walking backward so that he was forced to meet her eyes. "Why?"

"You've been watching CNN," he said. "You know damn well why. Despite what the tourist bureau says, there're people up in those mountains with guns."

"So? There're people in Puerto Norte with guns too. They're called soldiers, and from what I've seen on CNN, they're probably more dangerous than the rebel forces hiding in the jungle."

"You can spend the morning by the swimming pool, inside the hotel courtyard. You'll be safe there."

"You're kidding."

"No." He stepped past her, lengthening his stride.

"You barely speak Spanish," she pointed out, nearly running to keep up with him. "How are you going to communicate with anyone? How are you going to ask questions about Liam?"

He didn't even glance at her. "I don't know."

Kayla grabbed his arm and dug her heels into the sand, pulling him to a stop. "You're going to take me—*that's* how you're going to do it."

The heat of his temper flared in his ice-blue eyes as he glared down first at her and then at her hand still holding his arm. "You're *not* coming along."

"Because it's too dangerous?"

"That's right." He shook himself free from her

grasp and stepped past her again. But this time her words stopped him.

"That's a load of bull," she said hotly. "You don't want me to come along not because you're afraid *for* me—but because you're afraid *of* me. You can't handle the temptation, Bartlett. You think that something's going to happen between us."

Well, *that* may not have been the smartest thing to say. She could see the anger in the tension of his shoulders and back. She steeled herself for the explosion she knew would come.

He slowly turned to face her, pushing his hair back from his face. He looked at her, starting with the dark red nail polish on her toes and traveling all the way up to the top of her windswept curls, taking his merry old time on the way to study the lengths of her legs, the fullness of her breasts, the softness of her mouth. Finally he settled on her eyes.

She couldn't look away. She didn't want to look away.

"I *can* handle the temptation," he said quietly, dangerously. "And believe me, Kayla, you are one *hell* of a temptation. I figure after this is all said and done, I'll be ready for sainthood. Because nothing is going to happen between us."

"If that's really true, then let me come with you tomorrow," Kayla countered. "I'll be safer with you than I would be alone at the hotel." She had intended to play on his macho cowboy pride, but the funny thing was, she actually believed her own words. She *would* be safer with him. She *was* frightened at the thought of him leaving her alone. "Please?"

She could read nothing but coldness in the hard lines of his face. Somehow he'd taken all of his anger, all of his passion, all of his emotion, and pushed it deep down inside of him.

"Six A.M.," he told her. "If you're ready, you can come. But if you're one minute late, I'm leaving without you."

The black car.

It was at the edge of the parking lot, right next to their motorcycle. It was just sitting there. The windows were tinted—there was no way to see who or what was inside.

"What do we do?" Kayla murmured, glancing up at Cal. Her heart was racing.

"Go to the concession stand," he ordered her. "I'll get our boots and the bike and meet you over there."

"But what if it's the Special Forces Police? What if they grab you and drag you into that car and—"

"Please, Kayla." He took some of the colorful San Salustiano dollars from his pocket and pressed them into her hand. "Buy us both a soda. I'll be right there, okay?"

Her mouth was dry from sudden panic. "Cal—"

"Okay?" He turned her to face him, holding her chin so that she had to look into his eyes.

She found a certain stability there, a warmth and familiarity that calmed her, and she nodded. She should go to the concession stand and he would be right there. No one was getting kidnapped by the SFP. Not in broad daylight on a public beach. "Okay."

"Buy the sodas," he said again. "Make it look real. I don't want these boys to know we're on to them."

She nodded again, took a deep breath and forced a smile. "You want a cola or a root beer or something else?"

Cal smiled at her. "Whatever you're having."

Kayla reached for his hand. "Be careful." But he was already moving away, toward the bike and toward that sleek black, deadly looking car.

She forced herself to turn and walk toward the crude concrete shack that served as a refreshment stand. A pair of nearly identical-looking boys—they had to be twins—were behind the counter. One of them dug two cans of cola from an ice chest. They cost Kayla nearly ten San Salustiano dollars, which she thought was outrageous.

"It works out to be about three American dollars a can," said a man who was in line behind her. He spoke in English, and Kayla turned around to look at him.

"A sorry state of affairs, isn't it? Our economy has been nearly destroyed by the constant threat of violence between the government and the opposition party," the man continued. "I come down here all the time, to talk with the tourists, and each time the soda pop is a little bit more expensive."

He was strikingly handsome, with the dark hair and eyes that were native to the island. He was overdressed for the beach in a light-colored suit made of linen. Everything about him, from his well-styled hair to his expensive leather shoes, spoke of wealth.

Kayla smiled at him, and moved toward one of the brightly painted picnic tables that sat outside in the shade of a palm tree. Where was Cal? She searched for him, squinting against the brightness, her heart pounding as she couldn't see him and... Then she could see him. He was pushing the motorcycle far away from the black car. He was nearly up to the concession stand, and she quickly started toward him, carrying both of their sodas.

But the man followed her, opening his own can of soda with a crack. "I am Tomás Vásquez. I am connected with the San Salustiano Council of Tourism. Perhaps you would allow me to ask you several questions about your stay on our island."

Kayla knew Cal had heard the man's words as he reached for his soda. "Sorry, we're in something of a hurry today," he said in his smooth western drawl.

"Señor Bartlett, is it not?"

Cal froze. "Yes, it is."

"Perhaps we could walk, sir." Vásquez nodded slightly to Kayla. "Miss Grey."

How did this guy know their names? Kayla involuntarily glanced toward the black car. It hadn't moved.

"Ah, I see you are admiring my car," Vásquez said. He lowered his voice. "Yes, I have been following you. There is an important matter of which we must speak, but it is vital—for all of our safety—that we appear only to be discussing your stay as tourists on our island. Please, will you walk?"

He started toward the water, beckoning them to follow.

Kayla met Cal's eyes.

"Stay here," he said.

"No way!"

"I have no idea what this man wants from us."

"Neither do I—and that's exactly why I want to go talk to him. This is why we came to San Salustiano, Cal. Maybe this guy has some information about Liam."

"Then why would he approach us on the beach, where everyone can see us talking together?"

"He told me he comes here all the time," Kayla told him, "to talk to the tourists. What better place to contact us?"

Vásquez had stopped, and he stood watching them, waiting for them to catch up.

Kayla started toward him, but Cal caught her wrist. "Stay close to me," he whispered.

Vásquez looked out over the ocean, taking a drink from his can of soda. "It's amazing such a beautiful island should be the grounds for such a long and bloody battle," he mused. "Did you know that three years ago, during the worst of the fighting, a skirmish was fought right here, on this very spot?"

Cal shook his head. "No, I didn't know that. There was no mention of that in anything I've read."

"Often times the most fascinating of the stories are kept out of the newspapers and history books," Vásquez said. He turned toward them suddenly. "I know who you are and why you are here. I am given the names of people passing through customs, and Bartlett sounded familiar. I had the opportunity to access government computers earlier this afternoon, and sure enough, two years ago, a young American reporter named William Bartlett was killed in a terrorist explosion outside of Puerto Norte. It was a terrible tragedy." He took a deep breath. "However, being a disbeliever in coincidence, I checked the files more carefully and found that yes, William did have an older brother, Calvin Bartlett, who is, of course, you."

Kayla could see the tension in Cal's shoulders and neck, and she couldn't keep from reaching out and lightly squeezing his hand. He wasn't alone and she wanted him to remember that. As if acknowledging her silent message, he gently squeezed her hand too.

"In my capacity as a government official, I should scold you soundly for failing to let the authorities know that you came to San Salustiano to investigate your brother's death," Vásquez continued. "However, as a member of the Council of Tourism, I can appreciate your silence. The last thing *I* want is newspaper reporters and TV crews reminding the public that Americans were killed here in the recent past. That is why I have not mentioned your identity to anyone else.

"If you will allow me, I will assist you in your search for the truth. In a day or so I will escort you both to the place where the bus was bombed—

where your brother lost his life," Vásquez promised them. "The ruins of the bus have been left there as a monument to the dead. It will take me at least a day to get permission to travel into that area of the country, but if you will be patient, you will find such a visit helpful in understanding why the San Salustiano officials were unable to return your brother's remains."

"And what about the rumors that Liam was never even on that bus?" Cal asked quietly.

Vásquez seemed surprised. "I have not heard of such rumors."

Kayla couldn't believe that. She let her incredulousness show in her voice. "You've never heard of the legendary Americano who escaped from one of the prison camps in the mountains?"

The San Salustiano man took another long sip of his soda, then crushed the empty can in his hand. "I had heard talk of a mercenary American hired to fight with the opposition forces—a man well trusted and respected by the rebels. You honestly believe William Bartlett could be this man?"

"We don't know what to believe or who to trust," Kayla told him.

"If William Bartlett *is* still alive," Vásquez said as if thinking aloud, "and if he is this man so beloved by the opposition forces, then he could well provide the basis for the negotiations and peace talks this country needs so very badly." He drew in a deep breath and looked from Cal to Kayla, his gaze steady and filled with quiet determination. "We must begin to heal this country's wounds by trusting one another."

— 8 —

Cal knew the moment he stepped into his room that someone had been in there while he was out.

The shirts he had used to cover the video camera had been moved. They were neatly folded now and lying on top of the dresser, leaving the camera lens unobstructed. His cowboy hat had been delivered from the front desk—it lay on top of the neatly tidied bed along with several thick white towels.

"Oh, good, the maid's been here," Kayla said, coming into the room behind him, meeting his eyes just long enough to let him know that she, too, was aware they were being watched.

She sat down on the edge of the bed and picked up his hat. "I'm exhausted. I know you wanted to go out for dinner, but I'm ready to turn in early. My stomach's still upset from lunch, and ..."

Cal knew what she was doing. She was giving them an excuse to spend tonight in their separate rooms without arousing suspicion on the part of the people watching and listening in. That was good. That was *very* good. He wasn't sure he could handle pretending to be intimate with Kayla right now.

He sat down next to her on the bed, but he couldn't bring himself to touch her for the sake of the cameras. Not this time. "If that's what you want..." He gazed into her eyes, knowing she was thinking about their recent conversation with Tomás Vásquez, and about the question Cal had asked her on the beach after the man had left. *Do you trust him?*

"Why don't you order room service?" There had been such hope in her eyes as Vásquez had walked to his car and driven away from the beach. There was hope there still. *I don't know. Do you?*

I don't know. He hadn't answered truthfully. No, he didn't trust Vásquez. He didn't trust *any*-one. But he couldn't bear to see the hope in her eyes replaced by disappointment.

He nodded now. "Okay. Can I get something for you?"

"No. Thanks. If I want something to eat, I'll call myself." She stood up, moving toward the balcony doors. "I'll see you in the morning."

"I'll be right here if you need me."

Kayla stopped and looked back at him, meeting his eyes and smiling very slightly. "I know."

She stepped through the billowing curtain and disappeared into the deepening twilight.

Cal lay back on the bed and stared up at the ceiling. He'd be here if she needed him.

But what about if he needed her? And he did. God, he needed her. Desperately.

It wasn't just about sex. It was about the way Kayla could make him smile. It was about the way his entire being felt lighter when she was around. It was about the way he felt something was suddenly missing when she wasn't there.

Something like his heart.

Cal sat up quickly, pushing his thoughts away. He couldn't go in that direction. He *refused* to go in that direction.

He pulled off his boots and shirt. He didn't bother to cover the camera lens before he stepped out of his jeans and shorts and headed, naked, toward the shower. Let 'em look. He didn't give a damn about himself.

He turned on the water and stepped under the warm spray, letting it pound down on his head and pour over his face. He rolled his shoulders, trying to force himself to relax. But the tension wouldn't go away.

Sweet Jesus, today had been hard. And tomorrow was looking to be even harder.

———

"Which way?" Cal glanced over his shoulder at Kayla as he slowed the motorcycle to a stop at a fork in the narrow mountain road.

She loosened her hold around his waist and took the tourist map out of her fanny pack, comparing it one more time with the crudely hand-drawn map the San Salustiano woman had given her back in Boston.

The island was nearly one hundred and fifty miles long and about half as wide. The roads that wound up into the mountains were crumbling in disrepair. They'd been riding steadily upward all morning, stopping only for a quick lunch of bread and cheese that Kayla had thought to tuck into the bag behind the seat,

"Left. Definitely left." To her surprise, Cal hadn't argued when she'd told him she'd navigate. She'd been prepared to cite examples of her innate ability to tell direction. But he'd simply handed her the map.

He'd looked exhausted when they met out in front of the hotel lobby that morning, and she'd had to wonder if he'd slept as badly as she had.

She'd tossed and turned all night long, and when she *had* slept, her dreams had been filled with disturbing images—Cal's hard, powerful body pinning her to the bed as he gazed down into her eyes. Long, slow, soft, steamy kisses that made her melt, kisses that built in intensity and urgency until they were neither slow nor soft.

And then she struggled beneath him, asking him to stop. He didn't answer, and when she looked at him, his face had changed. He wasn't Cal any longer, and the fear nearly smothered her.

She'd awakened with a start, sitting up in bed, drenched with sweat. She'd spent the remainder of the night with the light on, slipping in and out of a dreamless, restless sleep.

Cal waited as she zipped the maps back into her fanny pack, and when she once again put her arms around his waist, he put the bike in gear, lifting his feet off the ground and repositioning them on the footrests.

He was wearing jeans and his worn-out cowboy boots again today, despite the fact that the tropical sun had already sent the temperature soaring into the nineties. A light-colored T-shirt hugged his upper body, and Kayla had the feeling that he wore it only out of deference to her. If he'd been alone in this heat, his shirt would have been off.

Her own T-shirt was folded and in her fanny pack. She wore only a bandeau bathing suit top with her shorts and sandals, and even then she was much too warm.

The road grew narrower, the jungle thickening almost discernibly on either side, as if seeking to swallow them whole. It was barely wide enough for a single car to pass through. Even on the motorcycle, Kayla felt vines and tendrils occasionally brush against her arms and legs.

The motorcycle's small engine whined as they climbed steadily uphill. Despite the fact that the road was shaded, Kayla felt a trickle of perspiration travel down between her breasts. She was glad Cal was wearing a T-shirt. If he hadn't been, their skin would have stuck together. As it was, his body heat and hard muscles brought back memories of the previous night's disturbing dreams.

"Right before we get to the top of this hill there should be another road off to the right," she told him, leaning closer to his ear to be heard over the engine.

He nodded once. "There's some kind of turnoff ahead."

It looked to be hardly more than a path, but as they got closer, it was clear that it had, at one time, been a road.

"Go past it," Kayla shouted. "If there's nothing else before the rise, we can come back."

They got to the top of the hill with no other turnoffs evident on either side of the road. Cal turned the bike around and coasted back down the hill.

"Let's take it."

Cal stopped the motorcycle at the beginning of

the road, and turned slightly in his seat to look at her. "Put your shirt back on. I don't know who we're going to run into out here, and I don't want to give 'em any...ideas."

"Such as the idea that since I've got my bathing suit on, I might want to go for a swim?"

He met her gaze evenly. "You know damn well that's not what I meant."

"Then say what you mean—don't talk in code."

"Cover yourself," he said bluntly. "You're underdressed."

"In your opinion. According to certain Pygmy tribes in Africa, I would be considered way *over*-dressed."

Cal cut the engine of the motorcycle and sudden silence surrounded them. "Maybe you're the one who should stop talking in code," he said quietly. "Why are you stalling, Kayla?"

Kayla looked at the narrow road and then into Cal's eyes. They seemed bluer in the deep shadows of the jungle. Bluer, and almost unbearably gentle. "I *am* stalling. I guess because I'm scared."

He didn't hesitate. "We can go back to the hotel."

She shook her head. "I'm not scared for *us*. I'm scared for *Liam*. For what we're going to find—or for what we're *not* going to find." She looked at the overgrown road. "No one's been down this way in weeks, maybe months. What kind of prison camp doesn't need supply trucks coming in and out?" The only answer she could come up with was not a good one: The prison camp—and Liam—were gone.

"Maybe there's another road in, one that's used more often." He reached to unfasten her helmet. "Come on. Put on your shirt and let's go see."

Kayla took off her helmet, and he held it for her as she pulled on her T-shirt. Her hair was damp from sweat, and she made a face as she slipped the helmet back on.

Cal smiled. "Brilliant idea, wearing helmets, huh? Especially since we're going to take this road at a whopping ten miles an hour."

"At least I know spiders won't drop off these branches and into my hair."

"Yeah, I think that's exactly what the helmet manufacturer had in mind." He jumped on the pedal that started the engine, then turned to give her one more look. "Ready?"

Kayla wrapped her arms around his waist. "Ready as I'll ever be."

Although Cal stayed in the very middle of the overgrown road, leaves and branches brushed past them like so many reaching, grasping fingers. Kayla held tightly to him, trying not to think about insects and snakes, trying not to think about rebels and government forces, trying not to think about Liam, locked in a foreign prison for two years, trying not to think at all.

But then suddenly they were in the middle of a clearing, the sun beating mercilessly down on their backs.

"What the *hell* . . . ?" Cal killed the motorcycle's engine as they stared around them.

The charred ruins of buildings and huts dotted the cleared area. It wasn't a prison camp—at least it wasn't the one that had been described to Kayla, with a huge stone building behind barbed-wire fencing. This looked instead as if it might have been some kind of town or village.

But it had been burned. Everything, including the jungle surrounding it, was blackened. It was as if the entire side of the mountain had been torched. But even so, already the jungle was reclaiming the earth. Tendrils of green had softened the edge of the burned area, and shoots were even coming up among the ruined buildings.

"What was it that old man in the pawnshop told us?" Kayla whispered. "That the Americano escaped from the prison camp and hid in a village, and the entire village was wiped out in retaliation?"

"He said that was just a story—made up to keep people in line."

"Maybe it wasn't just a story. Maybe it was true. It's obvious what we're looking at wasn't the result of someone's dinnertime grease fire," Kayla pointed out.

Cal gazed around, the muscle in the side of his jaw jumping. There were several rows of fairly fresh graves next to the ruins of what had to have been a church. The wooden crosses had been painted white, and they contrasted starkly with the charred ground. There were nearly three dozen of them, many of the crosses smaller, as if they marked the graves of children.

"Then where's Liam?" he asked, his voice raspy as he viciously started the motorcycle. "If these people died protecting the kid, where the hell *is* he?"

As if in answer, a gunshot rang out and a bullet smashed into the bike's side mirror, shattering it. Kayla didn't even have time to scream before Cal was reacting, gunning the engine. The rear wheel spun in the soot and ash, but then caught on the road and they leapt forward, toward the cover of the jungle.

Kayla clung to Cal as he pushed the bike harder, coaxing every last little bit of speed out of the aging engine. She closed her eyes, pressing her cheek against him, well aware that her back was a very large, very clear target. And the way they were sitting, a bullet that struck her could very well take both their lives.

She had brought Cal to San Salustiano, but she hadn't brought him there to die.

Another shot boomed, and Kayla closed her eyes even tighter, praying that it wouldn't be the last sound she heard. She felt a sharp tug on her upper arm and a blaze of heat. She'd been hit. Or had she? A pebble, thrown up by the bike's front tire struck her bare leg like the pellet from a BB gun, smacking her with a similar tug and burst of heat, hard enough to raise a welt. The smarting pain was good though—as long as she felt it, that meant she was still alive.

The jungle on the other side of the clearing swallowed them up as they roared along the overgrown road. Leaves and branches caught at them, tender green vines as sharp and stinging as whips as they raced past.

The speed at which the road zoomed by was both frightening and wildly exhilarating, the power of the engine mastered by the power in Cal's taut body. They surely were out of range and out of sight of the shooter, but he didn't slow down, and Kayla didn't want him to.

With a clarity born of the gunman's missed shots, she recognized the truth. She wanted Cal desperately. Emotionally, totally, in every way imaginable. Even physically. She knew without a single hesitation that she wanted to make love to this man. She wanted him to help conquer her fear, to banish it forever—or at least for as long as he held her in his arms.

She wanted to make love to Cal, and she liked going fast.

She liked it the same way she had liked Cal's kisses. It was dangerous, there was no denying that. One wrong move, and they'd be smeared across the cracked tarmac. Potential disaster was just a heartbeat away. But oh, how it made the adrenaline rush through her body. She felt alive—thoroughly, fabulously, breathtakingly alive.

She gripped Cal tighter with both her arms and her legs, trying to absorb the sheer power that seemed to radiate from him as the miles sped past. She knew she wanted more than he could afford to give, more than she could afford to take, and this reckless ride was a compromise. This ride was the only risk they could share.

But how she wished it were otherwise.

And then it was over. The motorcycle began to slow, the wild ride finally ending. Kayla lifted her head, looking up to find they were approaching what had once been an enormous wire fence. Barbed wire still straggled from the top, but the gate was half torn from its hinges, as if an angry giant had yanked it open.

Inside the compound was a stone structure in ruins that looked as if it had received many direct hits from mortar fire. The other outbuildings had been wood, and they, like the village, had been burned nearly to the ground.

The place was deserted. The only prisoners still inside were ghosts. And from what Kayla had heard and read about the long and bloody struggle for power in San Salustiano, there were no doubt hundreds upon hundreds of those ghosts among these ashes.

She shivered, reaching up to unfasten her helmet and— Her entire right shirtsleeve was soaked with blood.

Cal noticed it at the same time she did, and he cut the engine and was off the bike so fast, she barely saw him move. His helmet hit the dirt and he was crouched beside her. "Sweet Jesus, Kayla," he ground out through clenched teeth, "why didn't you tell me you were shot?"

"I was shot," she echoed faintly, staring down into his sweat-streaked face. "I didn't know."

Cal couldn't breathe. Half of the back of Kayla's shirt was stained bright red with her blood. He moved quickly, checking her eyes for shock, feeling her pulse at the base of her throat. Her eyes looked good, the pupils neither too big nor too small, but her pulse was racing. Was that a sign of shock? He couldn't remember. Her heartbeat seemed strong, and that could only be good. There was no sign of an exit wound, though, and that scared him to death. There was no way he was going to let those so-called doctors in the Puerto Norte hospital take her into surgery to remove a bullet from her back—or, God help her, out of her lungs.

"Are you having trouble breathing?" he asked her, cupping her face with his hands, gazing into her wide green eyes. He was willing her to be all right, and praying in double time. Dear God, let this girl be okay, and he would never ask for anything ever again. . . .

Kayla shook her head no.

Cal took his knife from its holster in his boot and, holding her steady, sliced upward through the thin cotton of her T-shirt.

"Hey!" she said, outrage tingeing her voice.

"Believe me, it was already ruined."

"Well, if it wasn't, it sure is now," she countered, "and on top of that, you cut my bathing-suit strap. Good job, Zorro."

Cal wasn't listening. He was carefully peeling the blood-sodden shirt from her back, bracing himself for the sight of a torn and angry-looking entry wound. But there was nothing. Only her smooth, pale skin, the fine blond hairs slightly damp with blood.

Where had all that blood come from?

He ran his fingers across the silkiness of her back in disbelief, turning her to face him and lifting the front of her shirt, still touching her, all sense of decorum vanished in his need to prove to himself that whatever wound she had received was not life-threatening. Her perfect breasts were whole and—

Her arm. Her upper arm was bleeding. And— of course—the pressure from their high-speed ride had kept the blood from flowing down her arm, instead pushing it down the back of her shirt.

He gently cut her sleeve, and there it was. A four-inch gash along the top of her deltoid muscle. It was truly no more than a surface wound, just a bad scrape that wouldn't even require stitches.

She wasn't going to die.

Cal sat back in the dirt, covering his face with his hand, focusing on breathing through the waves of relief that were threatening to drown him.

"Oh, my God." He looked up through his fingers to see Kayla taking her first good look at her bloodstained shirt, realization dawning on her face. She slid off the motorcycle and sat in the road next to him, holding the shirt in one hand and her bathing-suit top in place with the other. "You thought I was shot in the back?"

Cal nodded. "I thought..." He couldn't say it, couldn't say anything, couldn't do more than stare at her, his heart still in his throat.

She looked down at the wound in her arm. It

was still oozing blood. She met his gaze searchingly, her eyes wide. "How were we sitting that you weren't hit by this too?"

He reached for her, taking the T-shirt from her hand and tearing away the bloodstained half. He folded the clean part and used it to put pressure on her wound. "We were moving pretty quickly, and if the gun was fired at a distance, if the shooter wasn't using a rifle or long-distance weapon, if the bullet had lost velocity by the time it struck you—"

"*If?*" Kayla stared at him as he tied what was left of her shirt in place around her upper arm. "All those ifs..."

Still holding her bathing-suit top in place, she touched his arm as if needing confirmation that he, too, was in one solid piece. He couldn't help himself, and he put his arms around her, touching her shoulders, her hair, her face—the smoothness of her cheek, the softness of her lips. They were both trembling. Sweet Lord, this could have ended so tragically.

"We were lucky," he said harshly, closing his eyes and breathing in the sweet scent of her hair. "A few inches to the left, and right this minute you could very well be dying in my arms."

"I am," she whispered, her voice husky with emotion. "Cal, I am dying in your arms."

She closed her eyes and pressed her cheek into

the palm of his hand, lightly brushing the tips of his work-roughened fingers with her lips. When she looked up at him, when she opened her eyes, he could see a mirrored reflection of everything he felt, everything he wanted, everything he burned for.

Time stood still. Cal didn't move, he just gazed into those incredible eyes that were only inches away from his own, and let her see into his soul.

She smiled hesitantly, apologetically, just a quirk of her lips, and he felt his own mouth soften.

"I want you so bad, it's killing me," he said quietly, calmly, as if he weren't spilling his very guts right there in the dust for her to see.

She nodded. She already knew. Still, the words had needed to be said.

"I know it's wrong," he continued, and when she took a breath to speak, he gently put his thumb across her lips, silencing her. "And *you* know it's wrong, so don't go trying to make excuses, or to justify what this is we're feeling here."

He paused, letting himself absorb the powerful strength of their connection, giving himself a taste of what he knew he could not allow to be.

A taste . . .

He moistened his lips, and her eyes followed the movement, and he knew that even though it was wrong, he was going to give himself just that. A taste of Kayla Grey.

"This one's just for you and me," he whispered, watching his words register in her eyes, watching her understand why. "With no mistaken identities, and with no one watching, and even though we know it's wrong...."

Cal leaned toward her, and she closed her eyes and lifted her mouth to him. He kissed her slowly, taking his time, drinking in the sweetness of her lips, savoring the softness of her bare back beneath his fingers as he drew her even closer. He deepened the kiss, claiming full possession of her mouth, and her tongue met his in a languorous, bone-meltingly intimate dance.

He could feel the softness of her breasts crushed against him as she held him tightly. He knew she'd dropped her bathing-suit top. He knew he merely had to move his hand to cup the fullness of her breast in his palm. And he knew that he didn't dare allow himself that pleasure. Because he couldn't touch her without wanting to taste her, and that would be going too far.

Instead, he lost himself in the sweetness of her kiss, in the sheer, exquisite softness of her mouth as he kissed her deeper and longer, but still not harder, afraid to lose the tenuous grip he had on his control.

Because he had to remember that this kiss was only a taste.

Cal drew back slowly, leaving her as softly and

as gently as he'd started. Once again he took his time, lingering with feather-light kisses against her still-parted lips, knowing full well that this taste of paradise was going to have to last him a lifetime.

Slowly, she opened her eyes, and again he saw a reflection of everything he carried in his heart. This wasn't enough, this taste, this kiss. It wasn't enough and she desperately wanted more.

Sweet Lord, she was sitting in front of him, her breasts bare. She didn't move to cover herself, didn't move at all, and he couldn't help but look at her. She was exquisite—softly rounded porcelain skin, with rose-colored tips hardened into points of desire. He ached to touch her, taste her, bury himself inside her.

He met her eyes, letting her see his desire, letting her know that he, too, wanted so much more. But the knowledge of that fact was all he could give her.

He backed away, putting more space between them, and she drew in a deep, shaky breath.

"You are the most desirable woman I've ever known, but right now I need to keep my mind on Liam only, no matter what my body is telling me. And why I can't seem to resist you, even knowing the way you've been hurt in the past, even knowing the way my own brother felt about you . . ." He shook his head. He took off his shirt, quickly pulling it over his head and handing it to her. "Put this on."

Her arm hurt worse than she had let on, and as she tried to pull his T-shirt over her head, she winced. He moved to help her, gently guiding her injured arm into the sleeve, then pulling the collar over her head and helping her into the other armhole.

She gazed up at him as he pulled the shirt down across her stomach, covering her nakedness.

"What Liam and I had was different than you think." Her eyes brimmed with tears. "I *don't* love him," she admitted, "not that way. We were friends—close friends—and then he asked me to marry him and...I told him no, Cal, but he wouldn't listen. He told me to wait and think about it, until he got back from San Salustiano, but there was never anything to think about, because I didn't love him."

Cal straightened up, then reached down to help Kayla to her feet. He let go of her immediately, backing away to dust off the knees and the seat of his jeans.

"That's all right," he said quietly, turning to look at the deserted ruins of the island prison camp. "I love him enough for both of us."

—9—

"You sure someone's going to find this?" Cal asked.

"As long as it doesn't rain—and as long as someone comes out here to look. It's a long shot, but it's worth the thirty seconds it took to write it, don't you think?"

"What does it say?"

Kayla glanced up at Cal, brushing off her hands as she painfully straightened up from the place in the dirt where she'd scratched the message. "Roughly translated, it reads, 'We seek the truth. We are friends of the Americano.' I signed it 'Mike and the cowboy.'"

"Mike?"

She could meet his eyes only very briefly without getting light-headed from the memory of those incredible kisses. "Liam called me that. He thought the nickname for Mikayla should be Mike. And since he usually did what he wanted..." She shrugged.

"Well, I hate to break it to you, Mike, but I'm not a cowboy," Cal told her as he swung his leg over the motorcycle seat.

It was funny, actually. Or it would have been funny if her sense of humor hadn't been turned upside down and sideways when this man—this *cowboy*—took her in his arms and kissed her as if there were no tomorrow.

He was sitting astride the motorcycle wearing only his faded home-on-the-range-style blue jeans and his dusty brown cowboy boots, his broad, tanned chest gleaming in the sunshine, his dark, wavy hair tumbling over his genuine one-hundred-percent western American forehead, looking every little last fraction of an inch an authentic cowboy.

"I'm a cow*man*," he told her with a perfectly straight face, but with that now-familiar glint of amusement lurking in his gray-blue eyes. "There's a difference. The cowmen own the land they work. The cowboys just work it."

"Liam told me that you didn't just own the land—the land owned you. He was envious of you for those ties."

"He was *envious* of the noose around my neck?"

"He told me once that he felt as if he didn't belong anywhere." Kayla tried to explain. "As much as he loved Boston, it wasn't his home. And when he was with you at the ranch, he felt as if you could communicate with the mountains and the sky and the earth, and that he was out of the loop—that you spoke some language he'd never been taught. He laughed when he told me that he felt left out. He pretended it was just a great big joke, but I knew there was truth to his words."

"He was a lousy rider." There was a catch in Cal's voice. "For a kid born and raised on a working ranch, he was a *damned* lousy rider."

Kayla stepped toward him, drawn to him despite the knowledge that he wanted her to keep her distance. "And yet he kept at it. He even won that rodeo ring," she said. "Because he wanted to be a part of your world."

"Part of *my* world? I wanted to be part of *his*." Cal had an odd look on his face. "I always wanted to go to Harvard. I *dreamed* about going to Harvard. . . ."

"And Liam went."

"And I wanted to be a writer."

Kayla hadn't known that. Liam hadn't told her because no doubt Liam hadn't known either. Or had he? Had Liam taken on a life that wasn't quite his, forsaking his own dreams in an attempt to become the man his brother wanted him to be?

"During one of the last phone conversations I had with him," Cal said, "I was riding him because he was about to turn twenty-five. I teased him—told him it was high time he settled down and got married. I told him I was counting on him to get me some cute little nieces and nephews." He turned away from her slightly, pretending to be absorbed in the line that led from the handgrips to the front brake. But then he looked up, directly at her. "That was when he first told me about you."

"But you said he never spoke of me."

"I lied."

"What . . . what did he say?"

He was gazing at her, his pale blue eyes intense. "That the moment I met you, I would fall in love with you." He laughed, but there wasn't very much humor in it. "Damned if the kid wasn't right."

Kayla's heart was in her throat. Had he just told her . . . ?

As if aware he'd said too much, Cal started the motorcycle engine. "Come on, get on the bike," he told her gruffly. "There's no way in hell we're going back the same way we came in, and I don't want to get stuck out here, trying to navigate these roads after dark."

She put on her helmet and climbed on the bike behind him. Her shoulder ached as she put her arms around his waist. It ached, but not half as much as her heart.

"I think I'm falling in love with you too, Cal,"

she whispered, her words lost in the sound of the engine as they roared down the jungle road.

"There!" Kayla said. "Through the trees. Over to the right. There's definitely a light."

Cal saw it too. He could hear strains of music and the sound of voices echoing oddly through the darkness as he pushed the motorcycle along the mountain road.

They'd run out of gas.

He still couldn't think about it without feeling a surge of incredulousness. It was totally his fault. The man who'd rented him the bike had told him the gas gauge didn't work but that the tank was full. And Cal had been stupid enough to believe him, stupid enough not to double-check.

They'd been walking—and he'd been soundly cursing himself out—since sundown. It was already well past ten.

He'd wanted nothing more than to get Kayla safely back to the hotel. He'd wanted to wash out her wound, order her something to eat, tuck her safely into bed.

He'd failed miserably.

Of course, that was nothing new. This entire journey was a study in failure. The only thing he'd succeeded in doing was the one thing he'd tried desperately not to do: fall in love with the woman his brother loved.

Kayla was drawn to him. Cal knew that. He knew that she found the sexual attraction between them nearly impossible to resist. A part of him believed that it even overcame her fears of being intimate and that she would have made love to him right there on that deserted jungle road.

The pictures that swept into his mind were overpowering, and he had to shake his head to push them away.

She wanted him. And God knew he wanted her. Would it truly be so wrong to—

Yes. The answer came immediately. Yes, it would be wrong.

"Do we go in or keep walking?" Kayla asked.

He could barely make out her face in the dim light from the moon, but he couldn't miss the weariness in her voice.

She'd been shot. True, her wound wasn't life-threatening, but her arm had to hurt. Even a glancing blow from a bullet packed a wallop. Along with the gash on her arm, she probably had one hell of a bruise.

A burst of laughter drifted through the heavy brush, along with the fragrant aroma from an outdoor grill.

"What do you think?" he asked her.

"I think there's a fifty-fifty chance that whoever

they are will slit our throats and steal the motorcycle, but as long as they feed us some of whatever that is they've got cooking first, I'm not sure I'd mind."

Cal saw a slight break in the trees. It was a path leading down the hill toward the light. Kayla saw it too, and she turned down it. He followed, praying they weren't climbing out of the frying pan and into the campfire.

They weren't more than twenty meters down the trail, when he sensed more than saw or heard movement behind them. Someone had been out there in the darkness of the jungle, guarding the path.

Whoever they were, they moved slowly and quietly, not making an attempt to overtake them or threaten them in any way. At least not yet.

"Speak in Spanish," Cal said to Kayla in a low voice. "Tell whoever's behind us that we're Americans, we mean no harm. Tell them we're only looking to buy food and enough gasoline to get us back to Puerto Norte."

He heard Kayla's softly indrawn breath and knew that she hadn't heard the footsteps following them. But she spoke clearly and calmly, her voice carrying through the velvet darkness.

As they moved closer to the light, Cal could make out the outline of a building. It was no more than a shack, really, surrounded on all four sides by a clearing. Colorful paper lanterns were strung up in the front of the building, creating a festive feel to the rough-hewn tables and benches that surrounded a makeshift grill. The shack's windows had neither glass nor screens, yet a neon eagle flashed the logo of a familiar American beer.

As they stepped into the clearing, Cal realized that the music had been turned way down. He heard the unmistakable sound of guns—many, *many* guns—being locked and loaded.

Nearly all the men and quite a number of the women sitting at the tables had trained some kind of deadly looking gun on him and Kayla. And there were more—shadowy figures stepping out of the surrounding jungle, light glinting off their automatic weapons.

They weren't wearing the uniforms of the San Salustiano army. Rather, they were dressed like peasants—many of them literally wearing rags. But their guns were shining and well maintained. Despite their appearance, they were an army.

Kayla already had her hands held high, and Cal slowly lowered the kickstand on the motorcycle with one boot. Then he, too, moved slowly, cautiously, holding his hands in front of him, palms faceup, in a universal nonthreatening gesture.

As Kayla spoke in Spanish, Cal scanned the faces of the people sitting closest to them. No one so much as blinked or batted an eye.

He caught the words *Puerto Norte*, the words for food and gasoline. He heard her say something about the prison camp, about the golden-haired Americano, something about a brother, and, as if the move had been choreographed in advance, all eyes shifted, focusing on him.

One of the gunmen who'd been hiding in the jungle stepped forward, speaking quickly in a low, rough voice. He grabbed Kayla, and despite all the firepower aimed in his direction, Cal couldn't keep himself from moving toward her.

"Don't you touch her," he growled.

But a heavyset man grabbed him and pulled him toward the nearest table while another man stuck the dulled metal barrel of his gun into the soft area of Cal's throat, just underneath the hinge of his jaw. It might have been Cal's taller than average height, or it might have been the murderous look in his eyes, but two other men hurried forward to hold his arms despite the presence of the gun.

"It's all right," Kayla called to him quickly. "They just want to search us for weapons."

"Tell 'em to do it without touching you."

Her voice was low. "You know as well as I do that they can't do that."

Cal felt himself being patted down none too gently, and as his captors made a great deal of noise over discovering the holstered knife in his boot, he turned to look across the compound at Kayla.

She had closed her eyes against the roughness of the hands that swept her body. But as if she felt him watching her, she opened her eyes, turning to meet his gaze.

The connection was instant. Even there, in the middle of San Salustiano's equivalent of an outdoor roadhouse bar and grill, even surrounded by what had to be a significant and deadly portion of the militant rebel forces, the powerful bond between them snapped immediately to life.

"I'm all right," she told him soundlessly. "Do what they tell you to." Her eyes echoed her worry that he would, instead, do something to get himself shot.

One of the men searching him found his wallet hidden in his boot. He wasn't carrying any identification—he'd hidden it back in the hotel room for this very reason. His money could be taken and used, but his ID and passport were of value only if he weren't around to report it missing. He hadn't wanted to tempt any thieves into trying their hand at murder.

The money in his wallet was tossed onto a table. Many hands reached for it, but only one scooped it up. Cal followed that particular hand up a slim, muscular arm and found himself looking into the face of a young, dark-haired woman.

On second glance, he saw that he was mistaken. She wasn't quite a woman. She was really little more than a teenager—seventeen or eighteen at the most. She was dressed in black and carrying a submachine gun that was nearly as big as she was. Despite that, she carried it with total authority. Her face was sweetly pretty with the exception of a fresh jagged scar that marked her right cheekbone. That scar, and the bitterness and anger that sparked in her brown eyes, made her seem much older than she really was.

She waved the money at one of the men, and spoke in staccato Spanish. But then, to Cal's surprise, she turned back to look at him. When she spoke again, it was in clear, almost accentless American English. "This will cover the cost of a meal."

Cal was shoved down onto one of the benches, and he had to brace himself against the table to keep his head from being pushed into the unfinished wood. Kayla was pushed down next to him just as roughly. He reached for her, both pulling her close to him and, in one smooth motion, backhanding the man who had treated her so brutally.

He was slammed forward onto the table, and an ancient but extremely well-oiled revolver was nearly shoved up his nose for his trouble.

"Cal, no!" he heard Kayla say as the dark-haired girl gave a crisp order in Spanish.

The gun disappeared, and Kayla put her arms around him in relief.

The wound on her arm was bleeding through both the makeshift bandage and her shirt, but she was thinking of no one but him. "Don't you *dare* get yourself killed," she hissed through clenched teeth, shaking him slightly, her eyes bright with unshed tears. "Don't you *dare* do *any*thing like that again. They have guns, Einstein, and we don't!"

"Listen to your girlfriend." The girl sat down across from them as someone else placed plates filled with what looked like roasted fish along with refried beans and some kind of greens in front of them both.

"Who are you?" Cal asked.

"We are no one." Her smile didn't touch her darkly glittering eyes. "Or so our government would like us to believe." She fell silent for a moment. "You claim to be the brother of the legendary *Americano*."

Kayla leaned forward, eagerness in her voice. "Do you know him?"

The look in the girl's eyes was unreadable. She would have been one hell of an opponent in a poker game. "I didn't say that I did."

"Do you know where he is? Is he still alive? Is he all right?"

The girl ignored Kayla. "You claim to be his brother, yet you carry no proof of your identity. You expect us simply to believe you?"

"I have proof of who I am—back in my hotel room."

"Which is what you would say if you were only pretending, no?"

Cal let out a burst of air in frustration, knowing that the girl was right. Why should she believe him? "Let me go and get it. I can bring it back here—"

"You don't really think that we'd still be here, waiting for an ambush?" The girl laughed. "No, I can think of other ways that I would choose to die, Mr. Whoever-You-Claim-to-Be."

Kayla leaned forward again. "His name is Calvin Bartlett and he *is* Liam's brother. I know they don't look much alike, but they had different mothers. Cal was told that Liam was killed in a bus bombing two years ago. If his brother is still alive, if we still have cause to hope, please tell us now."

But the girl didn't give them any answers. "I'm sorry," she said, standing up. "We cannot put gas in your motorcycle. We have none to spare. In fact, we've taken what little oil you had—I'm sure you understand."

With that, she turned and strode quickly to the darkness that surrounded the clearing.

"Please," Kayla called after her. "Is he alive? Can't you even tell us that?"

But the girl had already stepped out of the light and disappeared.

$-10-$

No sooner had the girl with the machine gun disappeared than a murmur rippled through the crowd.

Cal leaned toward Kayla. "What are they saying?"

"There's a truck coming," she translated. As she watched, about thirty men, women, and children vanished into the jungle, taking their plates and cups with them, leaving most of the tables clear.

Four women rushed around with cloths, wiping the tables clean. Someone else turned up the radio. Trumpet music with a Cuban beat filled the air.

"Maybe we should get out of here," Cal said uneasily.

One of the women whisked their plates away from them. "Go," she spat out. "*Dejame!* Or blood will be spilled!"

Threat or premonition, that was one warning Kayla didn't need to hear twice. She stood up. "They want us to leave."

Cal moved quickly, taking her by the hand and pulling her toward the path that led up to the jungle road.

"The motorcycle?"

"To hell with it!"

But the people at the roadhouse didn't want the bike left behind. "Señor!" A teenage boy came chasing after them, pushing the motorcycle up the path. "Don't leave this here. They will find it and cause trouble!"

"Who will find it?" Kayla asked him. "Who does this truck belong to?"

"It is an army truck," he answered, pushing the bike harder up the hill, forcing them to follow. "There are soldiers searching the mountains tonight."

"Searching? For what?"

The boy looked at her as if she were a total idiot. "For you," he said. "For the two of you. The word from the shortwave radio is that two Americans are missing from Puerto Norte." He put on a burst of speed to push the bike the last few feet up the hill and onto the road. Turning to Cal, he gave him the handlebars. "They are using this excuse to search all of the towns and villages, all of the homes in the mountains. You must make it stop. You must let them find you."

The truck's headlights were blinding.

The oversized vehicle groaned to a stop twenty-five feet away. Orders were shouted in Spanish, followed by the sound of an entire platoon of feet jumping down from the back of the truck.

And for the second time that evening, Kayla found herself staring into the barrels of quite a number of very nasty-looking guns.

She lifted her hands, glancing over at Cal as more commands were shouted. "Brace yourself. We're going to be body-searched again," she warned him in a low voice.

His eyes narrowed in disbelief. "Why? If we're the ones they're looking for—"

"You *are* the ones we're looking for, Señor Bartlett." The voice was familiar, but its owner was standing with his back to the truck's headlights. Backlit the way he was, Kayla couldn't make out more than the shadowy figure of a man.

But then the man stepped forward, next to them, so that the light was shining on his face. It was Tomás Vásquez, the man they'd met at the beach. The owner of that sleek black car. The man who had agreed to help them search for the truth about Liam. He was wearing evening clothes—a black tuxedo and a crisp white shirt. Clearly, he'd been pulled away from some high-society party.

"A search is not necessary, Sergeant," he told one of the soldiers. "If you will take care of their motorcycle, they will come with me." He turned to Kayla, genuine concern in his eyes as he saw the blood still seeping through the sleeve of her shirt. Cal's shirt. "Are you injured?"

"I just ... I fell," she lied lamely, unwilling to tell him that she'd been shot. After all, she didn't know who had been shooting at them—one of the guerrillas, or one of the government soldiers. Trust me, he'd said, but she couldn't. Not entirely.

"Will you require a doctor?"

Kayla quickly shook her head. "It's not ... It's nothing, really."

"Perhaps you will allow me to have some bandages and antibiotic ointment brought to your hotel," Vásquez said in his gentle voice. "Infections are much too common with our humid weather."

"Thank you," Kayla said.

"My pleasure."

The soldiers around them were wearing a different uniform from the one she'd seen on the soldiers in town. These men were members of the Special Forces Police, she realized.

Liam had told her that he learned from his research on San Salustiano before leaving for the island that the Special Forces Police was little better than Nazi Germany's SS. The SFP, according to long-standing government policy, were allowed access into any structure on the island, regardless of whether or not it was a private home or business. The SFP could restrict the movements of any private citizen at any time for the purpose of national security. According to Liam, the list of civil rights violations committed by the group was dozens of pages long—and that had been over two years ago.

And here was Tomás Vásquez, supposedly of the Council on Tourism, giving orders to an SFP sergeant. It didn't make sense.

Vásquez led them around behind the truck to where his expensive-looking car was waiting. "I would have requested one of my men find you an extra shirt," he said to Cal, "but there are certain health risks involved with wearing a uniform this far out in the mountains." He gestured to the car. "Won't you get in?"

Kayla let Cal take the front seat. She climbed into the back, breathing in the new-car aroma that lingered among the leather-covered softly cushioned seats.

Despite the fact that it was the sort of car that often had a hired driver, Vásquez got behind the wheel himself. "The hotel called at nine, notifying us that you had left early in the morning and had not yet returned," he told them as he turned the key and the engine hummed softly to life. "We are always eager to avoid what could become an international incident, so I'm sure you realize how relieved we are to find you safe and sound so quickly."

"We ran out of gas," Cal said as the car moved smoothly along the jungle road.

Vásquez glanced briefly at Kayla in the rearview mirror. "An unfortunate event. May I recommend your staying in Puerto Norte and taking advantage of the resort's four-star amenities for the remainder of your visit?"

"You can certainly recommend it," Cal drawled.

The other man sighed. "But you will not follow my advice."

Kayla leaned forward. "Of course we will. I think we got a good enough taste of the mountains today and—"

"I have received permission to take you to the site of the bus bombing that took William Bartlett's life," Vásquez interrupted her. "I shall pick you up at your hotel tomorrow, say, ten o'clock?"

"All right," Cal said. He glanced back at Kayla. "Will you be up for that, or will you want to stay back at the hotel?"

She just looked at him, narrowing her eyes very slightly.

He actually smiled. "Sorry. Dumb question."

"I also found some information you might be interested in," Vásquez volunteered. "The intelligence reports I have had access to have mentioned an unnamed American man—your Americano. From the information I gathered, he was a mercenary who had joined forces with the rebels. He was believed to have been a former U.S. Navy SEAL. Quite a formidable enemy, apparently."

"Was?" Cal asked.

"Yes, he is dead."

As they reached the top of a rise, Kayla could see the lights of Puerto Norte in the distance. It looked sparkling and beautiful—a diamond in the darkness, not the capital city of a tiny country drenched with the blood of its people as it fought a decade-long civil war.

"He was fatally wounded when he was apprehended four weeks ago," Vásquez said, real regret in his voice. "I was on temporary leave at the time—I am afraid I only read the memos and reports of the incident." Vásquez shook his head. "You must put the last of your hopes to rest. The Americano was not your brother. And even if he were, he is no longer alive."

Kayla stood on the balcony, looking up at the city of Puerto Norte, the lights clinging to the mountain that rose up behind the resort hotel.

Cal leaned against the frame of the sliding glass door, just watching her.

She had cleaned out and bandaged the cut in her arm by herself, refusing his offer of help. She'd showered and changed into a loose-fitting dress. The fabric flowed gracefully around her—the effect made her look impossibly beautiful. Of course, in Cal's opinion, Kayla Grey had looked impossibly beautiful dressed in grubby cutoff jeans and his old, bloodstained T-shirt.

The streets below echoed with music and voices. Even though he hadn't made a sound, Kayla turned toward him, somehow knowing he was there.

"Someone's having a party tonight," she said.

He pushed himself forward, stepping out onto the balcony, even though he knew he was tempting fate by moving closer to her.

They had privacy to speak freely. He'd casually thrown the towel from his own shower over the video camera lens, and the radio was playing in his room, loudly enough to cover the sound of their voices from the balcony. And he'd checked this outside area thoroughly. It wasn't bugged.

"I called the front desk for a late dinner reservation and they recommended we order room service and dine in tonight," he told her. "That 'party' is a division of soldiers getting leave for the first time in four months. The concierge says they've been up in the mountains for at least that long. Apparently things can get a little wild, even in the hotel restaurant."

Kayla had been watching him, her eyes colorless in the dim light. "Cal, do you think he's dead?"

"Liam." He said the kid's name aloud though he knew for damn sure exactly whom she'd been talking about.

"There's no way Liam could've been mistaken for a Navy SEAL." She laughed, but it was a painful sound. "I mean, come on, really."

Cal looked at her, and his thoughts raced back to the last time they'd kissed. His body immediately responded, painfully. Here they were, talking about whether or not Liam was dead, and he couldn't keep his mind off his own selfish pleasure.

"He's not dead." Cal spoke the words experimentally, to see how they sounded. They sounded as if he were clinging hopefully to the side of a sheer cliff with the very tips of his broken fingernails.

"What if he is?" Kayla asked. "What if he were the man who died four weeks ago? Four *weeks* . . ." Making a small sound in the back of her throat, she turned away, gripping the railing. "God, if he was alive all that time, only to die four weeks ago, I'll never forgive myself for not getting here sooner."

She was crying. Cal could see the lights of the city reflected in the moisture on her face. He knew exactly how she felt, and he felt his own eyes fill with tears. He knew the exact sensation, the precise ache in her heart at the thought that Liam might have been alive all those months, with neither of them doing anything to help him.

"If he's dead, I hope to God he died in that explosion. If he didn't, then we're going to have to live with the fact that he spent nearly two years facing torture and God knows what and—" She couldn't stop a sob from escaping. "He was my *friend*. I didn't believe it when I heard that he died, but I didn't do anything about it. I should have come down here *then*, I should have—"

"Kayla." He took another step toward her, wanting to offer her comfort.

She didn't turn toward him. She just wiped her eyes fiercely with the heels of her hands. "You'd better go back inside," she said, her back still toward him, "because I need someone to hold me, and I know that's the last thing you want to do."

Cal closed his eyes. He couldn't comfort her with anything more than words—and there were no words he could say that would help. But if he so much as touched her, he knew he'd want to lose himself in her, to make love to her. And he simply wasn't strong enough to resist her. Not tonight. "Kayla, I "

"Hold me," she said softly. "Hold me, Cal, or leave me alone."

He did the only thing he could do.

He left her alone.

11

Kayla didn't see it at first.

It wasn't until she had stepped out of Tomás Vásquez's expensive car, until she'd gone a few steps into the underbrush.

And then, there it was. The bus. A twisted shell of burned and rusted metal.

There wasn't much of it left. She wasn't even sure she would have been able to identify that thing as a former mode of public transportation.

She couldn't speak. Cal, too, was silent, hands jammed into the front pockets of his jeans, a muscle working in the side of his jaw as he gazed at the wreckage.

According to the news accounts Kayla had heard at the time, forty-eight people—mostly women and children—had been instantly killed when the bomb went off.

Someone had planted flowers around the metal skeleton. They moved slightly in the late morning breeze, brilliant shades of red and orange; life among the death.

Cal turned and looked at her, and she could read his thoughts as clearly as if they were telepathically linked. Was this the place where Liam had died? If it was, then at least he'd gone quickly, immediately—no long-drawn-out, painful death by torture and malnutrition and God knows what.

She ached to pull Cal into her arms, but she knew he would only push her away.

Cal thought his brother was dead. Kayla could see it in the tightness of his jaw and shoulders, in the expressionless set to his face.

Kayla turned away as Vásquez cleared his throat. Today he wore chinos with a faded indigo blue polo shirt. It was the kind of faded color that cost seventy-five dollars new.

"There is something you both need to know," the man said quietly as they walked closer to the wreckage.

Vásquez touched the flaking rusty metal of the bus, then carefully brushed his hands clean, clearing his throat again. "I told you several days ago that I was unaware of any rumors concerning your brother's death. But this morning, when I checked into it..." He took a deep breath. "Mr. Bartlett, I now have reason to believe that your brother was not on this bus at the time of the deadly explosion."

Kayla couldn't move. Her feet had rooted her to this spot. She glanced sidelong at Cal, and saw that he, too, hadn't even blinked. But then he glanced at her, and she saw a flash of wildness in his eyes.

It was the closest thing to a plea for help that she'd ever seen or heard from him, and she didn't know what to do. She knew he didn't want her to touch him. He'd made that more than clear last night.

But then he surprised her. He reached out and took hold of her hand, breaking his own unspoken rule. And Kayla knew he did it as much for her as for himself.

He took a deep breath. When he spoke, his voice was deceptively calm. "Then where the hell *is* he?"

Vásquez didn't make any excuses. He looked first at Kayla and then directly in Cal's eyes as he spoke. "As far as I can tell, your brother was abducted by rebel forces and taken into the mountains prior to the explosion. From the information I've been able to gather, he had just interviewed the San Salustiano minister of defense. The assumption is that the guerrillas were hoping to uncover some military secrets. I've read a number of SFP memos, and it seems the situation was thoroughly out of control. The officials attempted to cover up the snafu by claiming William Bartlett had been on the destroyed bus. I think they fully expected the rebels to kill him."

"Did they?" Kayla asked.

She felt Cal's fingers tighten around hers as they waited for Vásquez's response.

"I don't know," he admitted. "I will do my best to find out more for you, but right now I just don't know."

"I don't believe him," Kayla muttered under her breath as they walked from the elevators to their hotel rooms.

Cal shook his head sharply, giving her a silent message with his eyes. Wait until they got inside the room, until he'd turned on the radio and covered up the camera lens. Then they could talk.

Still, Cal knew exactly what Kayla was thinking. Why would Vásquez tell them something that was potentially damaging to his organization and his very government?

But why would he lie? Unless he were deliberately feeding them false information. Or unless someone else might be deliberately feeding *him* false information...

He could feel Kayla's frustration—he was feeling similar tension himself. He wanted some answers.

If the rebels had kidnapped Liam the way

Vásquez had claimed, then who was the blond Americano that Kayla's San Salustiano refugee had seen in the government's military prison? Unless the mysterious American Navy SEAL who had allegedly been killed four weeks before looked remarkably like his brother...

But what was it Vásquez had said? He didn't believe in coincidence. Well, Cal didn't either.

He unlocked the door to his room.

"What's that?" Kayla asked. She started to reach down to pick up a folded piece of paper that had been shoved under the door, but Cal quickly covered it with his foot.

"Go onto the balcony and put your feet up while I get you something to drink," he told her.

She glanced up and saw that once again the "maid" had been in the room. The bed had been made, and the towel had been moved off the TV. The entire television console had been swiveled slightly, so that the camera hidden within was aimed toward the door.

As Kayla moved across the room, temporarily blocking the video camera, Cal dropped his key, then quickly bent and picked up both the key and the piece of paper. Concealing the paper in his hand, he moved to the bedside table and turned on the radio.

Someone—the maid no doubt—had put a fresh bucket of ice on the desk, with several bottles of mineral water chilling on top. He opened a bottle and poured some into a clean glass. Then he crossed toward the balcony, moving out of the camera's range.

But Kayla stood in the doorway, shaking her head. Putting a finger to her lips, she pointed underneath the white wicker table that was out on the balcony.

Sure enough, a new wire had been planted there, hidden against the intricate legs of the table. It was damn good that she'd looked. He handed her the glass of water and sat down at the table. "I'm hungry," he said for the benefit of the ears listening in. "Do you want me to order room service for lunch?"

"That would be nice," Kayla said, playing along. "Will you ask what the catch of the day is? I'm in the mood for fresh fish."

As he silently opened the piece of paper that had been left in his room, Kayla came to look over his shoulder.

At first Cal felt a flash of disappointment. It was a flyer from a shop downtown, nothing more than an advertisement announcing a sale. But then he realized which store it was. It was the store where they had bought the radio.

Another coincidence? He doubted it.

Kayla obviously doubted it too. "On second thought," she said, meeting his gaze, "why don't we go into town and have lunch at one of those little cafés by the harbor?"

Cal was silent as they walked into town. Their motorcycle had been appropriated the night before by the Special Forces Police and there were no cabs to be found. Kayla knew he was impatient to talk to the shopkeeper who had sold them the radio, but he was purposely shortening his stride so that she could keep up.

She didn't know how he was able to keep from running to find out what, if anything, the old man had discovered. "Do you suppose he's heard news of Liam?" she finally asked.

Cal glanced at her. He didn't answer right away, the hard soles of his cowboy boots making a soothing rhythm on the sidewalk.

He gazed out over the harbor as he spoke. "The summer before I turned eighteen, my granddad died."

It appeared to be a non sequitur, but Kayla knew if she waited long enough and heard him out, it would all make sense. "You mean the one who was your guardian."

He nodded. "Uh-huh. Although he didn't do much looking after us—didn't do more than sit and listen to the radio. He'd lost part of one leg to diabetes a few years before my father died, and..." He smiled. "He lost more than a few marbles at about the same time. The old man was a sly one though. Most of the time he didn't know where he was or who he was talking to, but he could fool you really well. Fooled the social services folks into granting him guardianship of Liam and me, which was just fine with me. But then, of course, Granddad went and died nearly six months before I was old enough—according to the eyes of the state—to care for Liam on my own."

He fell silent for a moment, remembering, lost in his past. And what a past it had been. He'd raised a child, starting at age fifteen, while putting in the long, grueling hours of a working cowboy. He was, without a doubt, the strongest man Kayla had ever met, both physically and spiritually. His power was written on the lines of his face, in the muscular curve of his shoulder, in the quietness of his gaze.

Kayla realized she was staring at him, but he didn't seem to mind or even notice. His eyes were distant, as if he were far, far away—or somewhere back in time.

"I still remember her name." He was talking more to himself than to her. "Corinna Pinter. She worked for the state, and she came out to the ranch and she took Liam away. Just like that. Took him to some lousy foster home clear across the county."

He was quiet again, and the only sound was the click of his boots on the sidewalk.

Kayla couldn't keep quiet. "What did you do?"

He glanced at her and smiled. "I turned eighteen, that's what I did."

"You mean you waited until your birthday and then—"

"Hell, no. I didn't wait for anything. One of my cowhands had done some hard time down in Kansas, and he knew a guy who knew a guy who dabbled in something he called the 'creative altering' of official documents. We took a little road trip south and my birth certificate, along with my driver's license and an entire slew of authentic papers were 'creatively altered.' Instead of being born November seventeenth, I now had proof that I'd come into the world in January of that same year. I was instantly eighteen. The Asylum town clerk backed me up, saying that it was her mistake—a typo. She said she'd added an extra number one to my month of birth on the papers that Corinna Pinter had gotten from the town files."

"So you got Liam back."

"Yeah, I got the kid back." His smile faded. "It doesn't seem likely, does it, that I'll be that lucky twice in one lifetime?"

Kayla didn't speak. There was nothing she

could possibly say. But she prayed with all her heart that the old man in the shop had good news for them—that he'd found out where Liam was hiding, that Liam was still alive.

Cal lengthened his stride as they crossed a road, and Kayla realized that they were approaching the shop.

Glass crunched under their feet. The small restaurant across the street had suffered a broken window. It had been broken from the inside, since the glass had sprayed outward, into the road.

All those soldiers had been in town last night. No doubt that little café had been the scene of a brawl.

Cal opened the door to the shop, holding it for Kayla, and they both went inside.

The old man was behind the counter. He greeted them by reaching down to a hidden shelf and pulling out a small box. He opened the box, taking a small gold object out and placing it on a black cloth spread on the counter in front of him.

Liam's journalism ring.

Kayla reached for it, but then stopped. It was dirty, the inlaid letters caked with some kind of mud or...

Blood.

"I didn't clean it," the old man said quietly. "I thought you would want to see it as it is."

"Thank you," Cal said. His voice sounded tight. "Where did you get it?"

"Last night many soldiers came into Puerto Norte on leave," he told them. "An old friend of mine likes to relieve them of their pay by engaging them in games of chance. My friend won this ring from one of the soldiers. This soldier told him he had cut it from the finger of a dead prisoner some time ago."

Cal didn't move. "Dead."

The old man nodded. "Yes. I am sorry. It appears I was wrong about the Americano. He was quite real."

Was.

"But the story I had heard had been altered—the story about the village being destroyed for harboring this man," the shopkeeper continued. "This soldier told my friend that the Americano did escape from the prison, badly injured. He *was* hidden in a nearby village and cared for by the people there, even though he was very sick. The SFP searched for him for weeks, and, through no one's fault, they discovered that he had been taken to this one village along the coast. The people were trying to smuggle him out of the country by boat."

Cal hadn't moved once while the old man spoke. He just listened.

"The Special Forces captain ordered all of the villagers into the town square. He lined up all the town officials and their families. He told the villagers that unless the Americano surrendered to them immediately, the village would be burned and their leaders would be killed. But no one said a word. And that was when the Americano came out of hiding.

"He was weak, hardly able to stand, but he would not let these people die for him." The old man drew in a deep breath. "But the captain ordered the executions and had the village bombed anyway. Even though this man had heroically given himself up, dozens of innocents were killed that day."

"And the Americano?" Kayla asked quietly, tears in her eyes.

"He was taken back to the prison and beaten. But he was a very strong man, and it wasn't until just a few weeks ago that he finally died. That was when our soldier acquired this ring."

Cal picked up the ring. "How much do we owe you?"

The old man hesitated. "I paid fifty dollars, American, for it."

"Thank you," Cal said. He took two crisp hundred-dollar bills and laid them on the counter. "For all your trouble."

But the shopkeeper was shaking his head. "The information I have given you is free. And if I can think of anything else that might be helpful—"

"Do you know the name of the SFP captain?" Cal asked.

"He is known as El Capitán Muerte by the people—Captain Death," the man replied. "He is an unassuming man, a gentleman—he doesn't look like the monster that he is. It is said he never wears the SFP uniform, and that he drives a car that cost more than the wages fifty families earn in five years' time."

Kayla looked at Cal, and saw that there was murder in his eyes.

"His name," the shopkeeper told them, "is Tomás Vásquez."

"Where are we going?"

"To the hotel," Cal told Kayla. "You're packing your things and I'm putting you on the next flight out of here."

"Excuse me?"

"You heard me."

"No, I didn't. I got caught in a bizarre time warp and heard the voice of some delusional Neanderthal who thought that just because he was bigger, he could order me around."

"Kayla, dammit, I don't have time for your crap—"

"When will you have time for my crap?" She put her hands on her hips and stepped in front of him, forcing him either to stop walking or step around her. He stepped around her. She chased him. "Will you have time for my crap after you do something stupid, like confront Vásquez and get yourself thrown in the very same prison Liam died in? Or maybe you'll have time after you're beaten into a pulp and killed too."

She was furious, her breasts rising and falling under her T-shirt as she struggled to keep up with him.

Sweet Lord, what was wrong with him? Liam was dead. Cal was almost one hundred percent certain that his little brother was dead, yet here *he* was, still alive and still lusting after Kayla. Dammit, couldn't he shut these feelings down for even a few minutes? For a moment of silence, a moment of respect for a man who had forsaken his own safety, a brave man who had died in an attempt to save others' lives . . .

He couldn't do it, not even for a few minutes.

All he wanted was to bury himself inside this woman, lose himself and all his pain in her sweet warmth.

With a groan he reached for her, and she went willingly into his arms, wrapping her arms around his neck and holding him close, so close it took his breath away.

"Please, let's get on a plane *together*," Kayla

whispered in his ear. "If Liam's dead, Cal, there's nothing more we can do for him."

"*If* Liam's dead."

She pulled back slightly to look up at him. "You don't still think . . ."

"God help me, I don't know *what* I think."

Kayla was gazing at him, her greenish eyes full of compassion and sorrow. "He's dead, Cal. That ring was *cut* from his body, for God's sake! Please, let's go home."

He pushed her hair back from her face, needing to touch her, needing her to understand. "It's all hearsay—stories, rumors, innuendo. There's no real proof."

"The ring—"

"Yeah, we have Liam's ring. It could have been . . . cut from his hand while he was still alive. Hell, maybe the blood on it proves that it was. Would he have bled if he were already dead?"

Her eyes were wide. "I don't know."

"I need proof," he repeated, "or there's always going to be a part of me wondering if maybe I went and gave up too soon."

She touched him, as if she had the same ache inside that he did. She ran her hands across his shoulders, placed her palms against his chest, touched the rough side of his face where his late-afternoon beard was already coming in. When she finally met his eyes, hers had filled with tears.

"Please, Cal, I don't want to lose you too. Don't you understand the kind of people we're dealing with? A man who could order the execution of innocent children...?"

"Ah, there you are! Just the Americans I was looking for."

Cal could see a sudden flash of fear in Kayla's eyes, and they both turned to see Tomás Vásquez's expensive car in the road alongside them.

"Of course, there are so very few Americans on the island these days, so that made my job a little bit easier."

Vásquez had opened his door and stood gazing at them over the car roof.

"However, I am afraid that this afternoon I am the bearer of bad news," he continued, his friendly smile turning into an expression of solemnity.

Cal released Kayla, stepping very slightly in front of her. He could feel the hair rising on the back of his neck. How could such a terrible killer—someone nicknamed Captain Death—appear so gentle and innocuous? It didn't make sense. But it didn't have to make sense. In all likelihood, this was the man who, directly or indirectly, was responsible for imprisoning and torturing and killing his brother—along with hundreds of other innocent people.

He felt Kayla grip his hand, clasping his fingers and squeezing slightly.

He read her silent message loud and clear: Don't go ballistic and kill this son of a bitch right where he was standing. Good plan. He wouldn't. At least not yet.

"I have news of your brother," Vásquez told him. He gestured to his car. "Come. Get in. We'll talk."

Kayla was right. They had to leave San Salustiano right away. But Cal would come back. He would charter a seaplane out of Puerto Rico and fly in at night, under cover of darkness. He'd find the San Salustiano rebels, talk to that girl with the big machine gun. She knew more than she had told them. He would find the proof that he needed to allow himself at least to sleep at night....

"We'd rather walk, thanks."

Vásquez shrugged and locked his car door. "That's fine too."

Well, that ruled out the possibility of Vásquez luring them to their untimely death. If he'd wanted to do that, he'd have insisted they get into his car, wouldn't he? It would have taken very little effort on his part, considering that the man was armed. He was wearing an expensive-looking sport coat, and it had opened slightly to reveal a small but deadly looking gun ensconced in a leather shoulder holster.

"I regret to have to inform you," Vásquez said,

looking thoroughly regretful as he joined them on the sidewalk, "that William Bartlett is indeed dead. I apologize for not being able to provide a more private place to tell you this, and for not delivering this news more tactfully, but I've found it best in this kind of situation not to delay. There is no easy way to share such tragic information."

Once again Cal found himself gripping Kayla's hand. "How did he die?" he asked, marveling at this man's effortless ability to sound so sincerely concerned.

Kayla was staring down at the street, as if afraid if she looked directly at him, Vásquez would read the fear and revulsion in her eyes.

"According to my investigation, it seems that a rescue mission was attempted—but the rebels had been forewarned. Thirty-eight of our soldiers were killed that day, along with your brother and several other hostages, including a cabinet minister's twelve-year-old daughter."

Vásquez reached inside his jacket, and Cal tensed, knowing that a gun was in there. But the man only pulled out a folded piece of paper.

"Your brother's death certificate." He handed the paper to Cal.

Cal looked down at the wrinkled paper he was holding in his hands. Liam's death certificate. This was the proof he'd been looking for. He opened it slowly, aware that the photo had been cut from Liam's passport and stapled to the document.

The words were all in Spanish, but Kayla was there, reading over his shoulder. She translated quietly. "Name: William Bartlett. Identification: Positive, from photo. Cause of death—" She broke off, and when Cal looked up, he saw she was crying. She took a deep breath. "Cause of death: Gunshot wounds. Date of death—" She looked up at Cal, wiping her tears from her face. "The ink's smudged—the date's been obscured."

"It was October," Vásquez told them. "Four months after the bus was bombed."

"Was it?" Kayla asked, and Cal knew what she was thinking. They'd just heard a story that had Liam alive up until just a few weeks ago. Was that why the date was smudged—because the story Váquez was telling was just another lie?

The only similarity between the two tales was that Liam was dead.

"This document was found in a box of papers due to be destroyed," Vásquez claimed. "I was lucky to find anything at all."

Cal nodded, gazing at the doctor's official signature, at the seal that had been stamped onto the thick paper.

Liam's death certificate.

He wished he were like Kayla. He wished he could cry—wished he could express his grief so openly and quickly. But he couldn't. It ran too deep, and once he brought it to the surface, he might never be able to keep it from destroying him.

He looked up at Vásquez. "What happened to his body?"

"That I don't know. I suspect it was left, along with the other dead and injured when the San Salustiano soldiers were forced to retreat. Apparently that area of the jungle wasn't recaptured by our troops for nearly two months. When our men went in, all the bodies were gone. It's believed that the rebels buried them—your brother included."

"How do I find out for certain?"

"You don't," Vásquez told him. "You take your lady friend back to your hotel and catch the next flight off the island. Your brother was killed by the rebels, Mr. Bartlett. Don't risk the same fate yourselves."

12

Liam was dead.

Kayla looked at Cal, and from the bleakness in his eyes she knew that the very last of his hope was gone.

Liam was really dead.

Kayla had called the airport from a pay phone, but the next available flight off the island—to any-where—wasn't until the next afternoon.

It seemed too long to wait, but even the char-tered flights were booked until the evening. And the tiny airport shut down tight at dusk. The best they could do was book two seats on the next flight out—and hope that the violence that was about to boil over remained at a slow simmer for just a lit-tle bit longer. There was one small charter service that suggested they arrive at the airport at five A.M., in anticipation that there might be some suddenly available seats on its six A.M. flight. It would be well worth the early wake-up call if they could get off the island that quickly.

They'd stayed downtown for most of the afternoon, walking and sitting by the harbor, watching the boats with their brightly colored sails. Cal was so quiet, Kayla felt as if she were totally alone. She gazed out at the water, letting herself grieve for Liam—for his wonderful, vibrant, brilliant life cut much too short, for all that he endured between the unknown number of months she'd been told about the bus explosion and the date that he truly did die.

Cal didn't say more than seven words to her all afternoon. He didn't touch much of his dinner either, and Kayla ached to say something, to *do* something, anything that would give him some small comfort.

She felt responsible. He'd been dealing with Liam's death. He'd lived with it for more than two years. But then she had to come along and give him false hope. Make him believe.

But Liam really was dead. All she'd given Cal was a fresh dose of pain and grief.

It was dusk by the time they returned to the hotel, and when they got there, the entire hotel was dark.

The concierge led them to their rooms with a flashlight, assuring them the problem with the electricity would quickly be taken care of. A major power line had come down as the result of an accident, but work was being done even as they spoke. Until the situation was rectified, the maid had brought candles and matches to their rooms, and did they want him to light those candles for them?

Cal just opened the door to his room and went inside as if he hadn't heard a single word spoken. Kayla told the man that they'd be fine, and followed Cal inside, wondering if everything she said to him would go as completely unnoticed.

She set her purse down on the desk, turning to face him.

"Maybe it would help if we talked," she started to say, but he cut her off.

"I want to be alone."

Go away. He didn't want her or need her. He didn't say those exact words, but his message couldn't have been more clear.

Kayla started toward the door to the balcony that connected their two rooms, but hesitated, not wanting to leave him there, alone in the dark.

Maybe he would use the opportunity to release some of his pain and grief.

But she knew he wouldn't. She knew this man pretty well, she realized suddenly. And just as sure as she knew her own heart was beating, she knew Cal was sending himself back into an emotional deep freeze—and this time he might never come out.

"Cal, God, I'm so sorry..."

He was silent. She couldn't see his face in the darkness, but she didn't need to.

"I really thought we were going to find him," she said. "And I know you did too...."

Nothing. Still nothing. But maybe he was crying. Maybe he wasn't speaking because he couldn't speak.

She could see the candles and matches that had been left in the room by the light from the last few streaks of the sunset that lingered in the sky. She struck a match, and the soft glow of light filled the room.

Cal sat on the edge of the bed, his eyes dry, his expression still so bleak.

She was the one who was crying.

"Please," he said, his voice devoid of all expression. He didn't even look up to meet her gaze. "Just go."

Kayla hesitated, lingering at the open door to the balcony. Cal had to look away. She was backlit by the red-orange sky with the candlelight caressing her face, her eyes filled with tears of compassion and remorse. She looked so beautiful, so *alive*.

He was still holding Liam's death certificate in his hands, and he looked down at it. He felt a wave of fury and sorrow churning inside him, rising like bile, and he forced it back down, refusing to let himself feel.

If he didn't let himself feel anything, then he wouldn't have to deal with the grief that was threatening to slice him in half. He wouldn't have to suffer guilt every time he so much as met Kayla's eyes—guilt over lusting for the woman his brother had loved, guilt over the way she could make him smile and even laugh, guilt over the way just looking at her could make him feel better.

And he wouldn't have to face the fact that he was alive, and Liam wasn't.

He sensed more than heard Kayla's movement as she finally went out the door.

He found himself listening for her, listening to the sound of her opening the sliding door that led into her room. He heard her step inside and—

She screamed.

It was a scream of pure terror, and it was cut short as if forcibly stopped. Cal's heart damn near quit beating and his blood froze in his veins.

He was off the bed like a shot, even before he realized she had been calling his name. He burst through the door to the balcony and into her room.

She hadn't lit a candle—she hadn't had time— but he could make out two shadows in her room.

Two shadows.

Sweet Lord, a man was in the room, and he was trying to hurt Kayla.

Cal couldn't tell if the man's hands were around Kayla's mouth or her throat. All he knew for certain was that no one—*no* one—was going to hurt this girl as long as there was any breath left in his body.

He grabbed the man by the collar of his shirt, dragging him away from Kayla, the force of his attack pushing her down onto the floor. She scrambled away as he slammed his fist into the intruder's face, sending him reeling.

The man hit the wall with enough force to knock a framed picture free, then bolted for the balcony door.

Cal gave chase, but whoever the intruder was, he'd been quick. When Cal got to the railing of the balcony, he was already on the ground, running through the darkness, disappearing around the corner of the darkened building.

Kayla.

Cal moved quickly back into her room.

She was still on the floor, sitting in the darkness with her knees up and her back against the wall. Cal knelt beside her, pulling her forward into the moonlight so he could see her face, see that she was all right.

She was trembling, but he more than half expected her to give him a shaky smile.

She didn't.

She looked shell-shocked, and she pulled away from him in fear, as if she didn't even recognize who he was. "Don't touch me!"

"Kayla, did he hurt you?" Cal asked her, a new blade of fear stabbing into him.

She didn't hear him. He might as well have been talking to the wall.

Sweet Jesus, when he'd heard her scream, he'd damn near gone into cardiac arrest. And now that the danger was past, now that his heart was beating again, it was sending an undeniable message with every pulsing surge of blood through his veins.

He would have died if anything had happened to Kayla. He would have fought to the death to keep her safe. He loved her—more than life itself.

The realization took his breath away, but he had no time to think about himself—he had to make sure she hadn't been badly hurt.

There were candles in her room too, and he lit them all, carrying one as he knelt back down next to her.

Her head was down, her arms tightly around her knees. But as he touched her gently on her shoulder, her head snapped up, and she began to scramble away from him.

Cal held the candle up and it lit his face. "Kayla, darlin', it's *me*."

She froze, gazing up at him. Something in her eyes shifted and focused, and he could see her sudden recognition. "Cal." She burst into tears and reached for him.

He barely had time to set down the candle before pulling her into his arms. She almost knocked him over with the fierceness of her embrace. He held her just as tightly, aware that he was shaking too.

As sobs shook her body, he reassured himself that she was all right. He touched her hair, her back, the softness of her arms, loving her with a desperation that made his chest ache. He felt like crying too—for Liam, who was no longer able to experience this odd, wonderful, uncomfortably alive sensation of having his heart in his throat.

Kayla's tears were slowing now, her breathing no longer quite so ragged, but still she held on to him tightly.

"I knew you would come," she said softly, finally lifting her head to look up at him. "I was just afraid you wouldn't hear me calling—"

"I heard you. Are you all right?"

Kayla wiped her eyes as she nodded. "All he kept saying was 'Silence! Be quiet!' He was trying to cover my mouth. And I—I just kept remembering..."

He pulled her closer. "I'm sorry."

She drew in a deep, shaky breath. "I'm definitely going to learn karate. I've wanted to for a while, but I kept putting it off and . . . Now I'm *definitely* signing up for a class as soon as I get home."

Home. They were heading home to the United States tomorrow, because they'd found proof that Liam was dead.

Cal closed his eyes against the sudden rush of pain.

Kayla gently touched his face. "Are *you* all right?"

He shook his head, sitting down on the floor next to her, his arm still around her shoulders. He couldn't let go of her. He didn't *want* to let go. "No."

"Liam's really dead," she said softly.

Cal felt his eyes fill with tears as he nodded. "Yeah. I think that he is."

He could feel her watching him, and he turned away.

Kayla could feel a fresh flood of tears fill her own eyes as she touched the side of his face again. His expression was like granite, unmoving and solid. "Cal, it's okay if you cry. You have every right to be angry. You have every right to grieve. Please, don't keep it inside, where it'll keep you from living too."

"I remember when he was about twelve years

old, a tornado warning came in over the radio," Cal said, staring out the open window at the moon slowly rising above the hills, his softly accented voice deceptively quiet. "He must've been home from school because he had a cold or something, and he was just hanging out, listening to a baseball game while I mended fences with the hired hands."

Kayla leaned her cheek against the broadness of his shoulder, wishing he would look at her, wishing he would let her share his pain.

"The sky was that telltale grayish-green that it gets when a twister's coming." He paused, finally turning toward her, finally meeting her gaze. "The kid knew he had to get down into the basement, to the little room that we use as a storm cellar, but he got it into his head that if he saddled up his horse, he'd be able to drive the herd up toward the back pastures and give 'em room to run from the danger of the storm. He could see 'em from the house, bunched up by the gate. The cattle knew damn well that bad weather was coming—they were nervous as hell—but the gate was closed.

"Liam ran out to the barn, but his horse was too spooked by the storm to let him saddle up. So he went bareback, charging out across that field, over to the gate. He got it opened, and nearly got trampled for his trouble."

He was still holding her gaze, as if it were a lifeline as he tried to blink back the tears that were threatening to overflow.

"That was about the time that twister came roaring through. It took out a couple of fences, but missed the house and barn. It missed Liam too, thank God, although he swears it passed right over him when he took cover in a ditch.

"I got home about five minutes later, and of course I found the storm cellar empty, and no sign of the kid."

"You must've been scared to death," Kayla murmured.

"No, not until I realized Liam's horse was gone. *Then* I was scared to death." He paused. "I saw that the gate was open, and put two and two together. It didn't take more than ten minutes to find him.

"I was madder'n hell, but he was so damn proud of what he'd done, I couldn't yell at him the way I wanted to. I knew that if I'd've been home, I would have done the exact same thing he did. I realized right then that he wasn't a baby anymore. I knew he had to make his own decisions and take his own risks, and that I wasn't going to be able to follow him around to make sure he always made the safest choices."

His battle was a losing one, and as Kayla

watched, his tears overflowed, running down his face. He didn't even try to wipe them away.

"I didn't think twice when he told me he was coming to San Salustiano," Cal told her, his tears falling faster now. "I didn't know where the hell it was, didn't even think to ask. Some kind of political trouble, he told me, and I figured no big deal. I teased him about the tough working conditions he'd have on a tropical island—girls in bikinis and piña coladas on the beach. I didn't even tell him to be careful. Next thing I knew, I've got a telegram telling me the kid's dead."

His voice broke, and he covered his face with his hands. Kayla could feel tears streaming down her own face as she tried to comfort him.

She couldn't say anything—she didn't want to say anything. His tears would help him to heal, so she simply held him while, as for probably the very first time in his entire adult life, Cal let another person see him cry.

Cal woke up in the middle of the night disoriented and confused. He was sleeping in a double bed with someone in his arms and . . .

Kayla. It was Kayla who was lying next to him, her leg thrown possessively across him as she slept.

Memories of the evening before came rushing

back. The intruder in her room. His incredible fear of losing her. His overwhelming grief.

Kayla stirred slightly, snuggling in closer to him.

She hadn't wanted to be alone—he couldn't blame her. She'd come into his room with him, and they'd locked the doors and he'd held her while she slept. Or maybe she'd held him while he'd slept. Either way, they both had been in need of a pair of comforting arms.

She shifted again, this time rousing. "Cal?"

"I'm right here," he murmured.

She pulled her leg off him, half sitting in the darkness. "Who's in the room?"

He sat up too. "No one. Just us."

"I was dreaming..." She took a deep breath. "Do the lights work? Can we please turn on a light?"

Cal tried the lamp that was next to the bed. "The power's still off." He reached for one of the candles and the matches he'd left on the bedside table and quickly lit it, holding it up so that the light shone around the room.

No one was there, of course. Kayla *had* been dreaming.

With a sigh of relief, she slumped down next to him. The tension in her shoulders was visible, and Cal pulled her into his arms. He could feel her heart pounding and he rubbed her back, trying to calm her down.

"You want to tell me about it?"

"The dream? No thanks." She laughed, a short burst of disgusted air. "Stephen King would've been proud. It was a master level nightmare of his caliber."

"I hardly ever remember my dreams," Cal mused. "It's funny, but back when I was a little kid, I used to have such vivid ones. Good dreams, though, not nightmares. I had this recurring dream that started with me falling, but then, before I hit the ground, I realized I could fly, and I just sailed over the ranch. It was amazing."

"I still dream that I'm falling." Kayla lifted her head to look up at him. "It scares me to death—I wake up shouting."

Cal smiled down into her eyes. "Next time, try to fly."

As he gazed down at her, he saw realization creep into her eyes. Awareness. Anticipation. It crackled around them like some living, breathing creature. She was in his arms, leaning against him. He was still stroking her back soothingly, trailing his fingers from the soft curls at the back of her neck down to the waistband of her shorts.

But then something changed. And even though he didn't touch her any differently, his soothing caress seemed electrified, and achingly, shock-ingly, intimate.

Her gaze flickered to his mouth, inches away from hers. "Are you going to kiss me?" she asked breathlessly.

Her blunt question surprised him, but he answered her just as honestly. "I was thinking about it."

Her eyes were wide and serious. But then she lifted her mouth the scant few inches that separated them. Her eyelids flickered closed as she brushed her lips against his in the gentlest of kisses.

Cal closed his own eyes, dizzy with pleasure at the sensation of her tongue softly outlining his lips, sweetly and so delicately taking possession of his mouth.

He groaned, pulling her closer and deepening the kiss, wanting more, *needing* more. Shock waves of desire exploded inside him as he kissed her even harder. He filled his hands with the softness of her body, letting his passion take control.

But then he pulled back, afraid he'd pushed too hard, gone too far.

He gazed down at her, his heart pounding just as loudly as it had earlier, when he'd fought her attacker. She was breathing raggedly too, and when she spoke, her voice was no louder than a whisper.

"In case you were wondering, that was definitely a come-on."

Cal had to laugh at that. Still, despite his smile, he knew that the sadness he could see in her eyes was mirrored in his own. "We've come full circle, haven't we, Kayla?"

She nodded, searching his eyes. "I don't want to push you into doing anything you don't feel ready for."

"Shouldn't that be my line?"

She looked so beautiful with the candlelight playing across her delicate cheekbones and gracefully shaped lips. She closed her eyes briefly, and her lashes looked ridiculously long and dark resting against her cheeks. And when she looked up at him again, he knew without a doubt that he could happily spend the rest of his life gazing into her incredible eyes. And still he didn't know...

"I think I'm a little worried about, well, what you've been through," he said awkwardly, "and—"

Kayla lightly pressed her fingers to his lips. "And I think it's time for you to stop worrying so much. I'm ready. Are you?"

"Yeah," he said. "I'm ready too."

Kayla searched his eyes—for what he didn't know. But whatever it was, she seemed satisfied, because she leaned forward and kissed him again.

Again he could feel every pounding beat of his

heart sending heat and desire pulsing to his fingers and toes. Sweet Lord, he wanted her.

And she'd made it more than clear that she wanted him.

The power was off in the hotel—the video camera was out of commission, but the listening device could very well still be operational, and there was no way he was going to make love to this woman with God knows who listening in.

He pulled away from her to turn on the radio, thankful it ran on batteries, tuning it quickly to the salsa music of the radio station on one of the neighboring islands. He set it near the planted bug, where it would mask their conversation and keep anyone from overhearing them. And, on second thought, he took one of the towels that the maid had brought and covered the camera lens. Just in case.

Kayla had turned to watch him, propped up on one elbow. If she had looked nervous, he might have turned away. But she gazed at him with such certainty and such incredible expectation in her eyes. He couldn't have kept from lying down next to her and pulling her into his arms if he'd tried.

She reached for him so willingly, her mouth so sweet, her arms so welcoming. She was a perfect fit against him, her legs intertwining with his naturally as he kissed her. He kissed her lazily, taking his time, content to lose himself in the softness of her lips. Lord, it felt so right. Holding her, kissing her like this was like coming home.

She slipped her hands underneath his shirt, and the sensation of her fingers against his skin was beyond description. With one swift pull he yanked his T-shirt over his head and tossed it onto the floor. She ran her hands across his back, sighing as if she got pleasure simply from touching him. She did. He could see it echoed in her eyes. She ran her fingers across his chest and down his shoulders and arms, smiling slightly as she met his eyes.

He tugged at her shirt, and she helped him pull it over her head. She was wearing that same nearly transparent black bra, and he allowed himself to look at her in the candlelight, lightly tracing the lace edging with one finger.

She was still watching him, and he looked into her eyes, silently asking permission to touch her. She smiled again, and opened the front clasp of her bra. Permission granted.

And then he couldn't keep from touching her, from cupping the exquisite softness of her breasts in his hand, from burying his face in her, from kissing, tasting, inhaling her.

Her legs tightened around his, her hips shifting to press against his and he was instantly, totally, frantically on fire.

He could feel her hands reaching for the buckle

of his belt, and his heartbeat nearly tripled in time. He'd never wanted a woman like this before. He never knew these feelings were possible. He'd never had a dream of his own be so close to coming true.

He forced himself to slow down. He was bigger than Kayla, stronger. God knows he wanted her, but he didn't want to hurt her. Or scare her.

He had to take it slow. He had to make sure she knew she was in charge, that she could stop him from going any further at any given moment.

He rolled onto his back, pulling her on top of him, giving her control. She sat up, straddling him, gazing down at him as she unfastened the top button of his jeans.

Somehow she'd taken off her shorts, and she was now wearing only a pair of black panties as she worked on unfastening his zipper. She smiled, almost shyly, and the effect was mind-blowing. Her body was sheer perfection. She was beautiful, and she was giving herself to him.

She finally wrestled his zipper down and he cried out with pleasure at the exquisite touch of her hand. But he wanted more.

He couldn't keep from taking hold of her knees and pulling her forward until they fit together perfectly, with only his shorts and her panties as a barrier between them.

She looked down at him and smiled again and

he knew that tonight he was going somewhere he'd never been before. Tonight his heart was involved.

And then, Lord, he wanted those clothes that were still between them gone. And she did too. She pulled back, off him, dragging his jeans down his legs, pulling his boots from his feet. He kicked himself free of his shorts, then reached for her, pulling her panties down the satiny smoothness of her thighs.

He had no protection. That knowledge damn near stopped him cold, but Kayla was there, reading his mind as clearly as if he'd spoken aloud. "In my bag," she said, pointing to the top of the desk where she'd left it earlier that evening.

He moved quickly across the room. Instead of searching through her fanny pack, he tossed it into her outstretched hands. She quickly found what she was looking for and held it out for him.

She sat on the bed, legs folded underneath her, watching him as he covered himself. The unabashed heat in her eyes was enough nearly to scald him as her gaze traveled down his body, taking in every little last detail of his nakedness.

Cal felt his heart kick further into overdrive. He was well aware that some women found him attractive. He'd seen desire and admiration in women's eyes before, but it had never affected him quite like this. He liked knowing that Kayla wanted him. It was a powerful feeling. A good feeling. He just wished he could measure whether or not she loved him as well by looking into her eyes.

He supposed he could tell her how he felt, gauge her reaction.

Or he could show her. That would be far easier—with far less risk involved.

She reached for him and he went into her arms, falling back with her on the bed. And then he could think of nothing but loving her, completely, totally.

He was lost in her kisses, lost in the silky smoothness of her skin, lost in the bottomless depths of her eyes, in the softness of her breasts, in the sweet curve of her smile.

She reached between them, encircling his arousal with her hands and smiling at the eruption of heat that had surely exploded from his eyes. He explored with his own hands as well, and nearly laughed aloud at her sudden intake of breath, at the way her body responded instantly to his touch.

Kayla was more than ready for him, sweetly slick with heat and need. She lifted her hips as if to meet him halfway, but he pulled back. This wasn't the way he'd wanted the first time to be. He wanted her to feel unconditionally and undisputedly in control as they made love. He wanted her on top, orchestrating each movement and determining every intimacy of their joining.

He wanted to look into her eyes and see no hesitation, not even a minuscule flicker of uncertainty or fear.

Again he rolled onto his back. She followed, as he'd hoped she would. The softness of her stomach was pressed against his arousal, her breasts against his chest as she kissed him. He ached to be inside her, but this had to be her show. She kissed his face, his chin, his neck, up to his ear, and then she whispered, "You're making sure I don't feel at all threatened."

"I'm trying, darlin'. Tell me what else I can do to help you."

She pulled back slightly to gaze down into his eyes, and Cal saw that her own eyes were filled with tears and something else—something warm and soft and impossibly tender.

Her voice caught slightly as she continued. "You know, if you're not careful, I could fall for you in a very big way."

His own voice suddenly barely worked. "Please do."

She shifted her hips and Cal caught his breath, feeling her softness and heat as she guided him into position beneath her. One upward thrust of his hips would bring him paradise, but he didn't move. He could feel beads of sweat forming on his upper lip and forehead, but still he didn't move. He just looked up into Kayla's green eyes and waited for her.

A small smile curved the corners of her mouth. "Of course you realize you've given me the power to totally torment you?"

Cal smiled back at her. If this was torment, it was the sweetest he'd ever known. She probably didn't realize that he would have waited for her for an eternity. A few minutes of teasing wouldn't make a speck of difference when compared to that.

He lightly ran his hands up the taut muscles of her inner thighs, holding her gaze. Her smile faded, and the fire in her eyes burned white hot as he touched her.

Slowly, she lowered herself on top of him. Slowly, he pressed himself upward until he filled her completely. And still she gazed into his eyes, and he into hers.

It was beyond good, beyond great, well past incredible, and it left amazing in the dust. It was a new experience and deserved a brand-new word, one that hadn't been thought of yet.

Cal felt himself smile, saw Kayla smile too. And he knew what it was he was feeling. There already *was* a word for it—and the word was a perfect one.

That word was love.

Kayla began to move slowly, excruciatingly,

deliciously slowly. He matched her pace, pulling her down on top of him to kiss her—long, penetrating kisses that mimicked the movement of their bodies. He felt her melt in his arms, heard her soft moan of pleasure as he continued the steady rhythm she'd started.

He couldn't help himself, and he picked up the pace. But she welcomed it, moving even faster, gripping him tightly with her legs. She kissed him one last time, then pushed herself up. She was magnificent—head thrown back, candlelight reflecting off her perspiration-slickened body.

Her breasts were peaked tightly with desire, and he reached for her, wanting to touch her, needing to touch her. She moaned and pressed herself more fully into his hand.

And then, like the first rumblings of an avalanche, he felt her shudder with the beginnings of her release. To his surprise and delight, she opened her eyes. Gazing directly at him, Kayla let go. And she swept him with her over the edge. He went with his eyes open too, burying himself in the sweetness of her body, and losing himself in the depths of her soul.

It was beyond good, beyond great, and well past incredible.

There was no doubt about it. It was love.

— 13 —

Kayla watched the flickering candlelight throw shadows around the room, listening to the slow and steady rhythm of Cal's breathing.

Making love to Cal Bartlett had been among the most powerful experiences of her entire life.

He'd been so gentle, so kind, so *careful* with her. More so even than was necessary. Not that she'd particularly minded. In her narrow band of experience, she'd never had a lover who had, well...*loved* her so completely. With Cal, she had felt cherished. It was an experience she hoped she'd get a chance to repeat. Often.

He shifted slightly, pulling her closer, her back against his front, murmuring something unintelligibly sleepy that ended with a wonderfully contented-sounding sigh as he cupped her breast with one work-roughened hand.

For the first time in her entire life, Kayla was precisely where she wanted to be. Well, maybe she didn't exactly want to be in San Salustiano, but she certainly wanted to be in this man's bed, clasped in his powerful arms.

She was where she wanted to be, but what about Cal? Would she forever remind him of Liam, thus bringing him more sorrow than joy? If so, she wouldn't be able to stay with him, no matter how much she wanted to. God, wouldn't that be the ultimate screw-up of her life? She'd finally found the one man she couldn't live without, only to find that the mere sight of her would forever bring him pain. The irony was outrageous.

But she was getting ahead of herself here. Before they could go their star-crossed, tragic, separate ways—if indeed that was what they were going to do—they first had to get safely out of San Salustiano.

She turned to face Cal, intending to wake him. She could see the glowing numbers of his watch on the bedside table. It was nearly four o'clock. They'd planned to arrive at the airport at five, on standby for seats on a filled six A.M. flight. It was time to get up and moving.

But Cal looked so peaceful in sleep, Kayla hesitated, watching him for a moment instead. His hair was tousled and his cheeks were dark and rough with the growth of his beard. He looked dangerously sexy, even with his flinty gray eyes closed.

Kayla had to moisten her suddenly dry lips as she remembered how he'd held her gaze as she'd exploded with passion, as he'd sent her spiraling over the edge. She also couldn't forget the way he'd let her hold him as he'd cried.

She bent to wake him with a kiss, but paused, listening hard. She'd thought she'd heard . . .

Tap, tap, scratch, tap.

There it was again.

She sat up, her sudden movement waking Cal, who was instantly alert.

"What is it?" he whispered. The room was dim with only the light from that single candle. The radio was still on, softly hissing white noise. The station had long since gone off the air for the night.

"Someone's on the balcony," she breathed.

Tap, tap, scratch. It was a little louder this time.

Cal slid out from under the sheet, reaching for his jeans. Kayla did the same, pulling on her shorts and shirt, taking no time to search for her underwear.

Kayla flicked the light switch. Nothing. The power was still out.

"Do you have the key to your room?" Cal asked almost silently.

The key to her . . . ? No. Wait, yes. It was in her purse. She quietly opened it and handed Cal the key to the room next door, questioning him with her eyes.

"I'm going to go through your room and try to get behind whoever's at that door," he said.

"You're kidding!"

"I'll be all right. You just be ready to run if they get that door open, okay?"

"No way am I going to retreat if you're attacking from the rear," she ordered fiercely. She pulled the lamp cord from the wall, holding the narrow part of the heavy ceramic base like a baseball bat. "Okay. Now I'm ready."

"Kayla . . ."

"Go," she whispered. "I'll be right here."

He hesitated. "Maybe we should both just clear out. We could just leave. Right now."

"Maybe we should find out who the hell wants to break into your room at four o'clock in the morning—knowing that we're in here, asleep."

Tap. Tap, tap.

Cal turned to look at the curtained door.

"Go," she said again.

He nodded. "All right, but you're coming with me."

Kayla couldn't argue with that.

Together, they crept out into the hallway and Kayla watched as Cal quietly unlocked the door to her room. Soundlessly, he pushed it open and they moved stealthily inside.

Following Cal's lead, Kayla stood behind him, hardly breathing, barely even blinking. When he was convinced there was no one waiting in the room for them, he moved toward the open sliding door and the balcony, and again she followed.

Kayla still clutched her lamp, but she felt far from prepared when she heard the soft murmur of voices on the balcony. Whoever they were, there were more than one of them. They were speaking in Spanish, but she couldn't quite make out the words.

Cal must have heard them too, and decided that he didn't like the odds. He motioned for her to back up, to head toward the other door.

And then the wind blew the curtain, and Kayla saw it. The dim moonlight glinted off an enormous and deadly looking automatic rifle one of the dark figures was holding at the ready in his arms.

His arms?

The curtain had moved back into place, and Kayla closed her eyes, trying to remember exactly what she had just seen.

If that was a man, it was a very young man, hardly no more than a child.... Or a girl. It *was* a girl—the teenage girl they'd met the day before yesterday, in the mountains.

Why was she trying to get into Cal's room? Obviously not to kill them. She'd had plenty of opportunity to do that up in the jungle, where their bodies would have disappeared without a trace. And obviously, she wasn't attempting a robbery. The balcony door to Kayla's room had been left open, with her clothes and her suitcase right there for the taking. Her things had been moved around, probably searched, but nothing taken. The girl and her friends had been in there, looking for something. Something or *someone* they no doubt hoped to find in Cal's room.

Such as Cal and Kayla, perhaps?

Kayla had to believe that they were members of the rebel army. And despite her youth, the girl was clearly in a position of command. Kayla had suspected this girl knew more about Liam than she'd let on. Maybe she had some information. Maybe she knew what had happened to Liam from the time of his abduction to the time of his death. Maybe she knew the location of his body.

"There's too many of them. I've counted at least four," Cal breathed into her ear. "I need to get you out of here."

"But I want to find out what they want."

"They want more hostages."

She shook her head. The rebels—or whoever they were—could have taken them hostage two nights ago.

"Kayla—"

She knew he wasn't going to be happy with her

for doing this, but she *had* to know. Before he could stop her, she stepped around him, through the curtain, and onto the balcony.

Cal was right behind her, but as three different muzzles of three different, very frightening-looking assault weapons were aimed directly at them, Kayla didn't need to glance in his direction to know he was angry. He was angry, but she knew he would have followed her directly into hell if she'd led the way there.

She may very well have just led the way there.

The two men with guns, and the man still crouched by the sliding door, trying to jimmy it open, all started talking at once. Kayla could pick out words and phrases she didn't quite like the sound of—talk of killing them now, talk of hidden agendas and identities pertaining to her and Cal's ability to materialize on the balcony the way they did. One of them actually thought this proved they were spies working for the Special Forces Police.

"Silence," the girl said brusquely and quite definitely. "Nobody's killing anyone."

Kayla saw that they'd found the listening device underneath the wicker table. It had been removed and crushed, like a cockroach. She took advantage of the sudden silence to point at it and whisper, "There's another in my room, but we have a radio in here"—she pointed at the sliding door to

Cal's room—"so we can talk inside without being overheard."

The girl gazed at her. "None of them are working. With the power out in the hotel, the transmitter is inoperable. We don't need your radio on to talk."

"Are you sure, because . . ."

"We are sure. We took out the power lines in order to talk to you without being detected."

"I assume that's why you're here," Kayla said hopefully. "To talk?"

"Got it." The man forcing the lock triumphantly slid the door open.

The girl didn't answer Kayla. Instead, she gestured with her head to one of the other men, and he went inside first, gun held at the ready. He stuck his head through the curtain a moment later. "All clear."

At the girl's obvious invitation with her weapon, Kayla went inside first. Cal was right behind her, and she risked a glance at him.

One of the men had a flashlight, and Cal's gaze was following the beam of light as it traveled around the room. The light lingered on the rumpled sheets of the unmade bed, on the brightly colored condom wrapper, torn in half and lying on the floor, on Kayla's lacy underwear and his T-shirt, lying where they had fallen. The room seemed to echo with the heat and passion of their recent intimacy.

The girl crossed toward the radio and turned it off. Then she reached down into the bedside table and removed the miniature microphone. She dropped it onto the tile floor and crushed it under the heel of her boot.

Cal looked down at Kayla. He was angry at the guns aimed in his direction, but he was right there beside her, one hundred percent.

"This is going to be okay," she said to him, realizing that for all he knew, they were about to be executed. The conversation had been going on around him in a language he didn't understand. "They just want to talk." God, she hoped she was right about that.

"If you're wrong—"

She reached for him. "If I'm wrong, I'll never forgive myself."

Cal held her tightly, speaking softly into her ear. "If you're wrong, I just want you to know . . . there's something I didn't tell you last night—"

"Sorry to interrupt this tender moment, but we don't have a lot of time." The girl spoke in her perfect, nearly accentless English, sitting down on one of the chairs by the sliding door. One of the men stood guard by that door, another stood at the other door, looking out the peephole at the hotel corridor. The third man—the one who'd picked the lock—had opened the front panel of the TV set, and was dismantling the video camera that had been hidden inside.

"My name is Marisala," the girl continued, looking from Cal to Kayla. "And you've already met Armando—you broke his nose, in fact, earlier this evening."

The man crouched in front of the TV set gave Cal a baleful glance. His nose was, indeed, bandaged.

"Since he was unable to deliver my message, I decided to deliver it myself." Marisala gazed at Kayla. "You are Mike, are you not?"

Kayla slipped out of Cal's arms, moving closer to Marisala, her heart pounding. She had been right. This girl had come with information about Liam. "Liam was the only one who ever called me Mike," she said. "You *did* know him, didn't you?"

"Yes," Marisala admitted. "I met him when he first came to Puerto Norte, more than two years ago. I was just a kid then."

She was just a kid now, but Kayla wasn't about to tell her that, not while she was carrying that very grown-up gun.

"We were told that he wasn't killed in the bus explosion," Cal said, "but that he was kidnapped by the rebels and taken into the mountains."

Marisala laughed. Her smile was sparkling, and it made her look like the beautiful teenage girl she was, softening even the harsh scar on her cheekbone. "Is that what they told you?" she asked. "That *we* took Liam?" Her smile faded as quickly as it had appeared. "They intercepted his fax to his newspaper," she told them fiercely. "They didn't like the story he wrote, didn't like the dirt he'd managed to uncover—didn't like his focus on the Special Forces Police and their arm-long list of human rights violations. *They* tried to kidnap him, tried to *kill* him. He came to me, badly injured—he knew I had friends who could hide him in the mountains."

She gazed at them steadily. "He sent messages to his newspaper and to his brother, but there was never any reply, and it wasn't until we were ambushed that I realized one of my own brother's friends was working for the government. Not only had the messages never been sent, but we were set up. In the surprise attack Liam was shot and badly wounded again."

"He was killed," Cal said. "I have his death certificate."

Marisala turned her luminous brown gaze to him. "He wasn't killed," she said. "He was hurt very badly, but he wasn't killed. He's a very strong man—he's been seriously injured twice more since then, but he's still very much alive."

— 14 —

"Alive?" Cal could hear the frozen disbelief in his own voice. "But the death certificate . . . It's signed by a doctor. . . ."

"No doubt it was a long distance diagnosis," Marisala said dryly. "The San Salustiano army doctors are quite good at doing that. The army lost nearly forty of its soldiers that day, but they never returned to claim a single body or to verify those men's deaths. We ended up burying them all."

Liam was *alive*. Was it possible?

"Where is he?" Kayla asked eagerly. "Is he hurt? Can you take us to see him?"

Cal put one hand on her arm. They weren't going anywhere with anyone. Not without some kind of proof. "How do we know you're telling us the truth?"

Marisala took a photo from her pocket. It was the kind that had been taken with one of those instant cameras. Silently, she handed it to Cal.

It was Liam.

He looked skinny and gaunt. He was sitting in a chair as if standing up would be too difficult a chore. His hair was long, but his face was clean shaven. Somehow he was managing to smile, a glint of his familiar happy-go-lucky humor showing in his blue eyes despite all he'd been through. He held a copy of a newspaper in his hands, front page visible to the camera. It was definitely Cal's little brother.

"That's today's paper," Marisala said. "I took this picture this morning." She had a scrap of the newspaper in her pocket and she unfolded it to show them the date. It was indeed the same front page Liam was holding, and it was dated that day.

Kayla had been looking over Cal's shoulder, but now she took the photograph from his hands, using one of the flashlights to examine it more closely. "It's him," she said, looking up to meet his gaze. "My God, it's really him!"

Cal had to sit down. Liam was alive. The kid was still alive. It didn't seem possible....

"Has he been with you all this time?" Kayla wanted to know. "Since he first came to you for help?"

Marisala shook her head. "No. Much has happened since then. After the so-called rescue attempt by the SFP, it was many months before I even knew if Liam was going to live or die, and more after that when he was very weak. And the entire time, the soldiers were searching for him. We had hidden him in a small village—my home village—on the west side of the island. It was on the water, and we'd hoped to smuggle Liam off San Salustiano by boat. But again we were found out. The Special Forces Police came into our houses before dawn. They searched everywhere, but Liam escaped into the jungle."

Cal's head was spinning, and he struggled to understand the San Salustiano girl's words. He felt like laughing, like crying—a jumble of emotions making his chest feel as if it were expanding. The kid was *alive*.

"The captain told us that he would kill half the villagers and burn the village if we didn't give Liam up within six hours," Marisala continued. It was the same story the shopkeeper had told them. Her voice grew thick with emotion. "Somehow Liam found out, and he surrendered, but El Capitán Muerte ordered the executions anyway. He made Liam and the rest of us watch as they murdered nearly fifty people. My father and little brother were among the dead that day."

"I'm sorry," Kayla murmured.

Marisala's dark eyes seemed to glitter. "That was when I vowed I would see my island free or die trying," she said quietly.

"The captain burned your village too, didn't

he?" Kayla asked. "We've heard a version of this story—but in the one we heard, Liam was taken to prison and beaten to death. We have his journalism ring—supposedly cut from his finger."

"He was taken to a prison in the mountains," Marisala agreed. "And beaten. But not killed. He was there for many months, and he will not speak of what he endured. I've seen some of his scars though, and I'm not sure I really want to find out. It was very bad, that I do know. But the last time I looked, he still had all ten of his fingers."

"How did he escape?" Kayla asked.

"He didn't," Marisala said. "My army infiltrated the prison and attacked from the inside about three months ago." She gave them a tight, satisfied smile. "It was one of the more successful operations of our little war. We had few casualties and we got Liam and the other prisoners out alive. *Mostly* alive. Liam was very nearly dead when I found him."

Cal watched Kayla's face, saw the flood of emotions sweep across it. She looked at him, tears brimming in her eyes.

"I feel like one of Lazarus's sisters," she whispered.

Lazarus's *sister*. Not his lover, or his wife.

She moved toward him and he enveloped her in his arms. He was crying too, just like a baby. Sweet Lord, he'd broken down twice in just a matter of hours, once because he thought the kid was dead, and once because he knew for sure that the kid wasn't.

Kayla clung to him, taking comfort from him and giving it in return. He buried his face in the sweetness of her hair, holding her close, wishing he could hold her forever.

A burst of realization hit him hard, and he felt suddenly sick. Dear God, not more than a few hours ago Cal had made love to the woman his brother wanted to marry. He'd given the kid up for dead, and given in to his own selfish needs. He released her slowly, jerkily, hardly able to move. What the hell was he doing? What had he done?

"The army retaliated by firebombing a village near the prison, but we had warning of that and got the people out in time," Marisala told them.

"But we saw all those graves..." Kayla said, wiping the tears from her face with both hands.

"A ruse to make them think their bombs killed our people. If they had no body count, they would retaliate again. So we painted crosses and buried leaves and branches to make them believe they won."

"How badly was Liam hurt?" Kayla asked. She glanced at Cal, but he couldn't meet her eyes. He couldn't even look at her.

"Badly. He is just starting to have the strength to walk again," the younger woman told her.

Kayla looked at the photograph one more time. "He looks...like a skinny Liam," she said with a laugh, smiling at Cal through her tears. "I can't believe this."

All of Cal's life he'd done his best to give Liam everything he could possibly want. The kid had been orphaned, he'd already been deprived of enough, so Cal had always bent over backward to provide him with anything his heart desired.

And what if the thing that Liam's heart desired was Kayla's love?

There's something I didn't tell you last night... Cal hadn't had a chance to tell Kayla. Sweet God, he was so glad he hadn't finished his sentence with the words he'd intended to say: *I love you.*

Because Liam was alive, and odds were that Liam still loved her too. How could he not? How could any man not love this woman?

It was better that she simply never know how Cal felt. It was better if she thought he didn't give a damn about her at all. Because, just the way he'd done many times before, Cal was going to walk away from his own dreams for his brother's sake.

But what about what he wanted?

What about finding heaven, finding peace and joy in Kayla Grey's eyes, then having to turn around and give it all back?

"I need your help getting Liam off the island," Marisala told them. "The SFP has renewed the search for him. We've got him hidden, but we've all learned that hiding's not the answer. He needs to go home, to America, and tell our story."

Cal squared his shoulders. "What's the best way to take him off the island?" he asked. "By boat? Or plane. I can pilot a small plane, and if I can charter one—"

"We have a plane," Marisala interrupted him. "We have three different planes at three different airstrips across the island. But no pilots. Liam told me you knew how to fly." She smiled grimly. "Of course, there's a catch. The SFP is aware of our planes, and is watching all the airfields at all times. There's too many of them for our guerrillas to take out without a full firefight."

"So what does that mean?" Kayla asked. "What can we do?"

"We either prepare for battle," Marisala said, "or—" She broke off, shaking her head. "Liam didn't like this plan. He forbade me even to suggest it." She looked up at them. "It would put you in a great deal of danger."

"My brother's already in a great deal of danger," Cal said evenly.

"Tell us," Kayla urged.

Marisala nodded. "You must go to Tomás Vásquez and ask him for his help."

"I want to go with you."

Cal barely even glanced at Kayla as he threw the rest of his clothes into his travel bag. "That would be stupid, and you know it."

Marisala's plan was shockingly simple—and shockingly dangerous. Cal would approach the "kindly" so-called Council of Tourism official, Tomás Vásquez, and tell him the good news—that his brother Liam was alive and well. Cal would ask for Vásquez's help getting Liam off San Salustiano. He would ask for help finding a pilot to fly an airplane that he had mysteriously been given access to. He would imply that the people who had led him to Liam didn't know that he had come to Vásquez for help—they had warned him against trusting anyone, but Cal knew Vásquez had risked his own career to help him once before, and therefore could be trusted.

Vásquez, of course, would be more than willing to provide Cal with a pilot. He would also let the plane take off from the tiny airstrip in the mountains, assuming that his pilot would simply land the plane—with its most wanted and highly valuable cargo, namely Liam—at the San Salustiano airport, thus delivering them all into the hands of the Special Forces Police.

Unless, of course, Vásquez knew that Cal and Kayla had figured out that he was, in fact, the notorious Captain Death of the SFP. Unless, of course, Vásquez knew that Cal intended to knock the pilot over the head and fly the plane to safety himself. Unless, of course, Vásquez figured it would be just as easy to toss Cal into one of his prisons and torture Liam's whereabouts out of him.

"Why should *you* be the one to risk your life?" she asked.

Cal paused, giving her a full, long look. His flinty blue eyes were distant, his face carefully guarded. God, was this really the man who had made such incredible love to her just a few hours before? His eyes had been impossibly warmer then. He'd nearly set her aflame with a single heated look. "Because he's my brother."

"But—"

"Kayla, stop. *I'm* the one who's going to talk to Vásquez, and *you're* the one who's not. You can talk at me until your face turns blue, but this time I'm not changing my mind."

"Talk at you," she said, repeating his words. "Nice, Bartlett. If I didn't know you better, if I weren't convinced you wouldn't do something so utterly moronic, I'd think you were purposely trying to antagonize me."

He turned back to his bag. "Why would I want to do that?"

"I don't know. You tell me. Guilt, maybe?"

He didn't say a word.

Kayla sat down on the bed, her heart wadded into a tight little ball and securely stuck in her throat. He *was* feeling guilty about the intimacies they'd shared. That had to be the reason for his coolness. "We need to talk about last night—"

He cut her off. "No, we don't. Don't worry, I have no intention of telling Liam. As far as I'm concerned, last night never happened."

Of all the things she'd expected him to say, that wasn't one of them.

Before she could find her voice, he turned to zip up his bag, as if the conversation were over.

"But it *did* happen. . . ."

Cal closed his eyes briefly. "What was it really?" he asked softly. "Emotional comfort. Physical need." He met her disbelieving gaze steadily. "In the scope of things, it was insignificant, Kayla."

Insignificant. The word echoed in her head as she stared at him, unable to comprehend what he was telling her.

"It didn't mean anything," he continued. "You know that as well as I do."

It didn't mean anything. No, she didn't know that. She hadn't realized. Kayla turned away before he could see the sudden rush of tears that had filled her eyes. Dear God, she'd given him her heart and her soul, and he thought it didn't mean anything.

"There'll be a taxi waiting for you outside the

hotel," Cal told her. "Armando will be the driver—
he's the man with the broken nose, remember?"

Silently, Kayla nodded. Cal had broken
Armando's nose, protecting her. How could she
forget?

"He'll take you up into the mountains, where
you'll meet Marisala and Liam," he continued.

"I should go with you," she interrupted him. "If
I'm there, Vásquez will believe the story. We
should tell him it was my idea to ask him for help.
Men like you don't ask for help. It'll make him suspicious if you do."

Cal picked up both of their bags and started for
the door. "That's a chance we're going to have to
take."

Cal glanced at his watch. He'd called Vásquez
and they'd set up a time to meet. Supposedly for a
midafternoon snack at the open air market down
by the harbor.

He'd watched Kayla get into the taxi. He'd resisted the urge to hold her close one last time. He
knew he'd hurt her. Insignificant. Lord, she'd
looked at him as if he'd struck her hard across the
face when he'd said that.

He saw Vásquez's familiar car approaching.
Sweet Jesus, there was so much that could go
wrong. Vásquez could have him arrested on the

spot. Vásquez could somehow find out which airfield and which plane they were intending to use to leave the country, and set up some kind of ambush there, preferring to risk the pilot's life to prevent Liam from escaping and telling the world about his two-year-long living hell on San Salustiano. Vásquez could somehow get his hands on Kayla, and use her as a hostage.

Cal dried the palms of his hands on the thighs of his jeans. He couldn't let Vásquez know he was sweating.

He watched the man—the notorious Captain Death—get out of his expensive car and set the alarm. He was wearing a light-colored suit, with leather sandals on his feet and a pair of designer sunglasses covering his eyes.

Cal knew he was a lousy actor, but now he had to put on a performance deserving of an Academy Award. Piece of cake. After all, he'd already done it earlier with Kayla.

"Don't be mad." The words were spoken softly from directly behind him. The voice could belong to only one person.

Cal turned around to face her. "Kayla, what the hell—"

"You can't be mad, because here he comes." She looked over his shoulder and smiled at the man approaching them.

Cal was furious. He should have known she

wouldn't do what he'd told her to. He didn't know what he'd been thinking. Follow instructions? Stay out of danger? He should have known she'd pull some stunt like this.

How could she knowingly put herself in danger? Didn't she know that there were no odds good enough to make him want to risk her life? Didn't she know that the thought of her thrown into one of San Salustiano's barbaric prisons was enough to turn his blood to ice.

No. She didn't know. She didn't realize it, because he'd tried—and succeeded—in convincing her that he didn't give a damn.

She took his hand and held on tightly. "You need me," she told him softly, "whether or not you know it."

He knew it. He knew it all too well. But there was no time to try to tell her that, no time to talk. Vásquez was upon them.

"Let us walk," he said as a way of greeting. "Down by the water."

They walked in silence, Kayla still holding tightly to Cal's hand, until they were well out of range of listening ears.

"Thank you so much for coming to talk to us," Kayla said before Cal could speak. Her voice shook as if she were holding back tears, and sure enough, her eyes were filled. Whether it was fear or some other emotion, she was entirely convincing. "I asked Cal to give you a call because, well, to be honest, we didn't know where else to turn."

"I am honored you would trust me enough to come to me," Vásquez murmured.

"Cal didn't want to," Kayla told him, "but I talked him into it. You see, we've received word that Cal's brother is still alive."

Cal watched Vásquez's face as Kayla fed him the entire story. The midnight contact from mysterious people who had a photo of Liam. The pilotless airplane waiting at one of three possible mountain airstrips. Their assigned task of finding a pilot, and waiting at a contact point with that pilot for a taxi to pick them up. Then and only then would they be told Liam's whereabouts and the location of the plane. The plan was to time it just right and leave at dusk, vanishing into the darkness of the night.

The man didn't blink, didn't twitch, didn't give any guilty jumps or starts.

"We need a pilot," Kayla told him. "We need someone who can fly a small plane to take us all off the island, and we need him *soon*. We're supposed to meet the taxi in front of the hotel in less than an hour. This man must not carry a weapon or be wired for surveillance in any way, because the people who have Liam are dangerous and very suspicious. Please, can you help us?"

"What you are asking me to do might be seen

by some as a very serious crime against my country," he said solemnly. He drew in a deep breath and looked at Cal. "However. I will help you. You must promise me in return that when your brother regains his health he is allowed to return to our island to help negotiate a peaceful understanding between the opposition and the current government."

Cal shook hands with the devil as he lied, "I promise."

"You will have your pilot," Vásquez promised in return. "He will meet you in half an hour in front of the hotel."

Kayla was silent as they approached the small airplane.

So far everything had gone smoothly.

The pilot had arrived at the hotel, and the three of them had gotten into a taxi that took them deep into the twisting, turning narrow roads of Puerto Norte. They had switched cars more times than Kayla could count in an attempt to lose anyone who might be tailing them. Somewhere down the line, the pilot had been temporarily put to sleep with a well-aimed blow to the side of his head.

Armando had traded clothes with the man. With a baseball cap pulled down over his eyes, he looked enough like the pilot from a distance. At least, they hoped he did. The pilot, interestingly enough, had been carrying his own parachute. Armando suspected he'd been ordered by Vásquez to flush the fuel tanks and exit the plane, leaving the Bartlett brothers and Kayla Grey alone on a plane destined to plunge into the sea.

But it wasn't going to happen that way.

Cal was going to fly the plane, and Vásquez was going to let them leave, thinking their deaths were guaranteed.

It was only a matter of minutes now before they met Marisala and Liam at the plane.

The jungle road opened up into the sudden brightness of a tiny clearing that must have been the airfield. Kayla could see another car, bumping and jostling too as it moved swiftly across the field, heading toward a small battered-looking airplane that had been covered with a camouflage tarp. She reached across the backseat and touched Cal's hand.

The look he gave her told her much more than she was sure he'd intended. She wondered if he could see her own fear as completely. She wondered if he could tell just from looking into her eyes that she loved him.

He glanced away from her, out the window at the other approaching car. Liam was in there. He looked back at her. "Don't tell him."

Kayla knew exactly what he was talking about.

He didn't want her to tell Liam that she'd slept with Cal. She pulled her hand away. "I have to. You don't think I'd just never tell—"

"I meant not right away. Don't tell him right away. Let's wait until he's been checked by a doctor. Wait until we know he's okay."

She nodded.

"Thanks." The car jerked to a stop, and Cal threw the door open. Four or five men she didn't recognize swarmed over the plane, removing the tarp, readying it for takeoff.

Kayla knew they had to do this quickly. One of the men reached into the car for their luggage. Another took her arm, helping her up and into the rickety-looking airplane.

She could see Liam as Marisala helped him out of the other car, his golden hair gleaming in the sun. She watched Cal embrace him, watched him effortlessly take Liam into his arms, watched Liam reach back to touch Marisala's hand one last time.

And then Cal carried Liam into the plane. God, he was so skinny and his hair was so *long*. He was weeping, and Kayla realized that she was crying too.

Cal set Liam down next to her, and she pulled him into her arms. He met her eyes for only a fraction of a second before he settled into the pilot's seat and started the engine. It was only the briefest of moments, but it had been long enough to tell her all she needed to know.

The iceman was back. Cal was giving away no more secrets with his eyes.

The plane rattled and shook as it raced down the bumpy little airstrip, but Cal pulled it up and into the sky. He swung out, directly over the ocean, away from the mountains, away from the city of Puerto Norte.

"Hey, Mike." Liam smiled at her through his tears.

"Hey, Bartlett." Her own smile was just as soggy.

"I guess you met my brother."

Kayla nodded. Yes, she'd met his brother.

Insignificant.

The word was following Kayla around, popping into her head when she least expected it.

She'd been back to work for nearly four weeks now. She would have thought the hurt would have begun to fade.

It hadn't.

But life went on, and her life was no exception. She was busy. She made a point to be busy. Too busy to think—except when unwanted thoughts popped into her head.

Liam was hard at work on a book based on his experiences in the jungles of San Salustiano. He'd already written a series of articles for the *Boston Globe* that had created quite a stir. He was living in a tiny apartment in Back Bay, his furniture and possessions pulled out of storage. Cal hadn't thrown anything of Liam's away. Cal hadn't even sold his brother's town house—but it was rented to a tenant who held a lease until December.

Cal had helped Liam find this place, helped him move his stuff in, made sure his brother was well on the road to good health.

And then Cal had returned to his ranch in Montana.

He hadn't even said good-bye to Kayla. Or maybe he had. Maybe that long look and that nod he gave her the last time she saw him had been his way of saying So long, it's been fun.

Kayla trudged up the stairs to Liam's second floor apartment, wondering why she'd agreed to meet him there. They'd spoken often and at great length since Liam's stay in the San Juan Hospital, since they'd taken him off San Salustiano. Liam had apologized to her for making her wait so long before accepting her refusal of his marriage proposal. It had taken only one smile for him to acknowledge what she'd known all those long months ago—they were, and always would remain, friends and only friends.

Liam had told her about the San Salustiano prison. He'd told her terrible things, awful things, and she knew he hadn't told her everything. But that was okay. She was still keeping secrets from him. After all, she'd made a promise to Cal.

Cal.

The last time she'd seen Cal, he'd been here.

His shirt had been off in the warm autumn sunshine as he'd carried boxes of Liam's books up this very flight of stairs.

Insignificant.

Why hadn't she challenged him? Why hadn't she thrown that word back in his face? Why hadn't she kissed him with all the passion in her heart and soul and dared him to use that word again after reminding him of what they had done, what they had felt, what they had shared?

Okay, so maybe for Cal it had been nothing more than great sex. Maybe love didn't have anything to do with what he'd felt when he'd held her in his arms that night. But whatever it had been, it *hadn't* been insignificant.

Liam opened the door before she was even halfway up the stairs. He had gained some weight and was walking with only the aid of a cane, but his hair was still long—a souvenir from his trip to hell. He wore it back in a loose ponytail.

"Gee, can you take any longer to climb up here?" he asked, looking down over the railing at her.

"I'm tired," she said. "I can't seem to catch up on the work I missed all those weeks I was away."

"Funny, Cal said almost the exact same thing."

"You spoke to Cal?" Kayla couldn't hide the longing in her voice, and Liam gave her a long, appraising look.

"Last night." He followed her into his apartment and closed the door behind him with his foot, then led the way into the kitchen. "We talked last night. He sounds like crap. Kind of like the way *you* sounded when I called you this morning. Tired and angry for no apparent reason. Coffee?"

He held out a mug and Kayla shook her head. He poured himself a cup from his coffee machine and leaned against the kitchen counter, sipping it and watching her over the rim.

"He told me what happened between you guys in San Salustiano," he said quietly. "He told me he slept with you, Mike."

She met his gaze levelly. "I didn't tell you because he asked me to wait to talk to you until he did. I figured as soon as he said something, you'd tell me and we could talk."

"He didn't say much about it, just that it happened and that he wanted me to know. In fact, he seemed kind of surprised that I didn't already know."

Kayla had to smile at that. "I don't think he expected me to do what he asked and not tell you."

Liam grinned. "Guess he got to know you pretty well, huh?"

She sat down at his kitchen table and fidgeted with the salt and pepper shakers. "Remember how I told you I was afraid I'd never be able to be intimate with anyone ever again?" she asked. "And remember how you told me I would know when the time was right?"

"Yeah," Liam said. "I guess the time was right, huh?"

"No. It wasn't about timing at all. It was about who I was with. It was about Cal, about the way I felt about him."

Liam put down his coffee mug, his movements quick and impatient—so different from Cal's seemingly slow and careful gestures. "The way you felt. Are you going to be more specific, Mike, or should I start to guess?"

"Love," she said, knowing she couldn't hide anything from Liam. Sooner or later, he *would* guess. "I fell in love with your brother, Li."

"I'm devastated." He sounded anything but. "Here I've just gone and spent two years in the jungle pining away for you..."

"You've spent the past four weeks pining," Kayla said astutely. "My guess is you're not missing the jungle or the prison in the mountains. So let's see... What does that leave? A woman?"

"You want the awful truth?"

"The whole truth and nothing but," she said.

"God, it's embarrassing to say it out loud, it sounds so sleazy, but..." He took a deep breath. "There was a San Salustiano girl I had this incredible thing for, and don't go all feminist on me for using the word *girl,* because that was what she was. A girl, Mike. A little kid. When I first met her, she was only fifteen. *Fifteen*. She turned seventeen a few months ago—man, seventeen's hardly any better."

"Marisala," Kayla guessed.

"Bingo. I taught her to speak English. You don't want to know what I *wanted* to teach her. . . . But I didn't touch her, I didn't even kiss her, not even once. I was a monk, Mike, I swear. *Madre de Dios*, I hope she's all right. You should see her use an AK-47. She's . . . amazing." Liam's voice got softer. "I'm worried sick about her."

"Do you love her?"

"Hell, I don't know. All I know is she saved my life more than once. I owe her, Mike, bigtime."

They were both silent for a moment, then Kayla spoke. "Liam, about Cal . . ."

"Yeah?"

"He doesn't know . . . you know . . . that I love him." Her voice faltered. "And I think his feelings aren't exactly mutual."

Liam sat down across from her at the table. "Mike, let me tell you a thing or two about my brother."

Insignificant.

Dust rose up in the rearview mirror of the rental car as Kayla turned down the long drive that led to the Bartlett ranch.

Her heart was in her throat. This was definitely the most foolish thing she'd ever done.

What exactly was she going to say to Cal? But, hey, she'd come this far before to try to save Liam's life. It was only fitting she should make the same effort for her own life.

And then she was there. She pulled up in front of the ranch house, parking alongside Cal's truck. She could see Thor standing on the porch, watching her, ears alert, checking her out. The dog gave a single bark, turning to look over his shoulder at the house before returning his full attention to Kayla.

She climbed out of the car and stood looking over the top as Cal opened the screen and stepped onto the porch.

He didn't say anything. He just gazed at her. God, he looked so good, dressed in his jeans and cowboy boots. His dark hair was damp with sweat and dented where he'd worn his hat, probably during the long hours he'd worked that morning.

"Hi," she said. It wasn't a brilliant opener, but it was the best she could manage under the circumstances.

He leaned one shoulder up against one of the columns that held up the porch roof, his flinty blue eyes appraising her coolly.

"Do you think," he said in his gentle western drawl, "that if I call the airline right back, they'll let me cancel my reservation on tonight's flight to Boston without making me pay the penalty?"

Kayla's heart was in her throat. "You were coming to Boston? Tonight?"

He nodded. "Damn, but I am glad to see you." His voice broke slightly, so slightly, Kayla was left wondering if she'd imagined it. But she wasn't imagining the fact that he'd pushed himself forward, off the porch, and was now walking toward her, his long legs quickly covering the ground between them.

She moved too, and then the waiting was over. She was in his arms. He was glad to see her. Coming to him wasn't the most foolish thing she'd ever done.

His mouth landed firmly on hers and she lost herself in the sweetness of his kiss. But only temporarily. Instead of holding him close, she pushed him away.

He tried to pull her close again, but she pushed him away again, refusing to be sidetracked. She lifted her chin and looked him in the eye. "*Insignificant* wasn't the word *I* would've used to describe that night."

He had to laugh. "Don't tell me you came all this way just to tell me that."

"I love you," she told him. "And it *wasn't* insignificant."

His eyes looked warm, and so impossibly vulnerable as he looked back at her. "I know," he said softly. "I don't know why you love me, but...I don't give a damn why anymore. You know, in my life, I can count on one hand the things I've done purely because *I* wanted to do 'em." He touched her face, running his fingers through her hair. "One of those things was making love to you. And you're right. It wasn't insignificant, hell, it was everything and anything but. I was just trying to make it easier for you to walk away by telling you that."

"I may have walked, but I went in a full circle, because here I am again." Kayla had tears in her eyes, and she didn't wipe them away. She didn't care if he saw them.

Because there were tears in his eyes too. "Yeah," he whispered. "Here you are, aren't you?" He kissed her again.

"Were you really coming to Boston?"

"I couldn't stay away."

She held him tightly. "Why did you leave?"

"I thought it would be best—"

"Best for whom? Not me. And certainly not you."

Cal nodded. "Yeah," he said. "It wasn't best for me." He smiled ruefully. "It's kind of hard to break the habit, but I was going to fly into Boston tonight and come banging on your door at four o'clock in the morning. How's that for doing something purely for me?"

"I would have loved it."

"I was going to sweep you off your feet the second you answered the door and tell you that I love you," he continued.

Kayla's voice caught. "I would have loved that too."

"And then I was going to tell you to pack your things because I was taking you back to Montana with me. I was going to tell you that we were going to get married as soon as possible."

He lifted her chin, about to cover her mouth with his in another bone-meltingly delicious kiss, but she stopped him with one hand on his chest and a dangerous glint in her eye. "Tell, not ask?"

Cal smiled. "You know, you still owe me a steak dinner."

"Tell, not ask?"

He was grinning at her. "I am *so* damn glad to see you—"

"Tell, not ask?"

"Yeah," he finally answered her. "Tell. Not ask. I figure since it's the first and last time I'm ever going to be so damned selfish, I might as well go big. Because I figure that from the moment you say that marrying me is okay with you, I'm going to spend every waking moment of the rest of my life giving you everything your heart desires."

He bent to kiss her, and this time she didn't push him away.

"Marrying you is okay with me," she whispered, her lips a breath away from his.

Cal smiled and kissed her.

About the Author

Since her explosion onto the publishing scene more than ten years ago, Suzanne Brockmann has written more than forty books, and is now widely recognized as a leading voice in romantic suspense. Her work has earned her repeated appearances on *USA Today* and *New York Times* Bestseller lists, as well as numerous awards, including Romance Writers of America's #1 Favorite Book of the Year—three years running in 2000, 20001, and 2002—two RITA awards, and many *Romantic Times* Reviewer's Choice Awards. Suzanne Brockmann lives west of Boston with her husband, author Ed Gaffney. Visit her website at www.suzanne brockmann.com.